Crossing The Cosmic Horizon

Anthony Fontenot

Published by Anthony Fontenot, 2024.

This is a work of fiction. Similarities to real people, places, or events are entirely coincidental.

CROSSING THE COSMIC HORIZON

First edition. December 2, 2024.

Copyright © 2024 Anthony Fontenot.

ISBN: 979-8230704768

Written by Anthony Fontenot.

To my amazing readers,

Thank you for joining me on this thrilling adventure! Your enthusiasm and support mean the world to me. I'm honored to have shared this journey with you, and I hope you enjoyed the ride as much as I did.

Thank you for being part of my literary universe!

THE WARLORD'S AMBITION

Zorvath, the formidable warlord of the WfRX, stood before the massive window of his throne room, gazing out at the galaxy he sought to conquer. His piercing yellow eyes burned with an inner fire, fueled by his unyielding ambition. The dim light of the room danced across his scaly, crimson skin, casting an ominous glow on the proceedings.

Xarath, his trusted advisor and a member of the subservient Kraelion species, entered the room with a deep bow. "My lord Zorvath, the time of conquest approaches."

Zorvath turned to face Xarath, his deep, rumbling voice dripping with menace. "The galaxy will soon tremble before me. All will bow to the might of the WfRX."

Xarath knelt, his eyes downcast. "But at what cost, my lord? The innocent will suffer, worlds will burn..."

Zorvath's expression twisted in rage, his clawed hand rising as if to strike. "Silence! You dare question the will of a WfRX warlord?"

Xarath looked up, fear etched on his face. "I fear for the future, my lord. You were once a just and fair ruler..."

Zorvath's laughter was cold and mirthless. "Fool! I am the embodiment of the WfRX spirit. Conquest, domination, and destruction are my birthright."

Xarath backed away, horror in his eyes. "I will not stand by and watch you bring destruction upon the galaxy."

Zorvath summoned his guards with a curt gesture. "Take him away. Throw him into the darkest dungeon. Let him rot."

As Xarath was dragged away, he cried out in desperation. "You will never be satiated, Zorvath! Your hunger for power will consume you!"

Zorvath's expression twisted in rage as he watched Xarath disappear into the darkness. His whisper was barely audible, but it sent shivers down the spines of those who heard it. "I will show him... I will show them all... The galaxy will burn, and I will reign supreme."

The darkness seemed to closing in around Zorvath, fueling his ambition and hunger for power. He turned back to the window, his eyes burning with an inner fire as he gazed out at the galaxy.

"The time of conquest is upon us," he whispered to himself, his voice echoing off the cold, metallic walls of the throne room. "The WfRX will reign supreme, and all will bow to our might."

As he spoke, the stars seemed to twinkle in agreement, their light dancing across the darkness like a chorus of approval. Zorvath's heart swelled with pride and ambition, his mind racing with the possibilities.

He turned to his loyal lieutenant, Thrakos, who stood waiting by the door. "Summon the war council," Zorvath growled, his voice low and menacing. "We have a galaxy to conquer."

Thrakos bowed deeply, his scaly skin glistening in the dim light. "As you command, my lord," he said, before turning to disappear into the darkness.

Zorvath watched him go, a cold smile spreading across his face. The war council would be assembled soon, and the plans for galactic domination would be set in motion.

CROSSING THE COSMIC HORIZON

The WfRX would stop at nothing to achieve their goal, crushing all opposition beneath their heel. And Zorvath, the mighty warlord, would lead the charge.

The galaxy trembled at the thought, unaware of the horrors that were to come. But Zorvath knew, and his heart sang with anticipation.

For in a universe where only the strongest survived, the WfRX would reign supreme. And Zorvath, the greatest warlord of all time, would be the one to bring them to glory.

ZORVATH PACED BACK and forth in front of the war council, his eyes blazing with excitement. "We will conquer the galaxy," he declared, his voice rising to a crescendo. "And we will do it with... with... (he paused for dramatic effect) ...giant space squids!"

The war council stared at him in confusion. "Giant space squids, my lord?" Thrakos repeated, his voice laced with skepticism.

Zorvath nodded vigorously. "Yes, yes, it's genius! We will genetically engineer giant squids to pilot our spaceships. They will be the ultimate warriors, capable of navigating the complexities of space combat with ease."

The war council exchanged dubious glances. "But, my lord," ventured one of the council members, "squids don't have the cognitive abilities to pilot spaceships. And even if they did, how would we control them?"

Zorvath waved his hand dismissively. "Details, details. We will figure it out. The important thing is that we will have giant space squids, and they will be unstoppable."

The war council looked at each other, unsure of how to respond. They had seen Zorvath's temper before, and they knew that it was not wise to question his plans too closely.

But Thrakos, ever the loyal lieutenant, spoke up. "My lord, I think this plan has... merit. We can make it work."

Zorvath's face lit up with excitement. "I knew you would see it, Thrakos. You are a true visionary. Together, we will make the galaxy tremble with fear."

The war council nodded in agreement, trying to hide their skepticism. But as they left the meeting room, they couldn't help but wonder what other bizarre plans Zorvath had in store for them.

Meanwhile, Zorvath was already making plans to implement his giant space squid strategy. He summoned his chief scientist, a brilliant but slightly unhinged WfRX named Dr. Vraxxis.

"Dr. Vraxxis," Zorvath said, his eyes gleaming with excitement. "I have a new project for you. I want you to genetically engineer giant squids to pilot our spaceships."

Dr. Vraxxis's eyes widened in surprise, but then a look of manic enthusiasm crossed his face. "Ah, my lord, that's a brilliant idea! I can see it now - giant squids, piloting our ships, destroying our enemies... it's genius!"

Zorvath grinned, pleased that someone shared his vision. "I knew you would see it, Dr. Vraxxis. Make it happen."

And with that, the fate of the galaxy was sealed. The giant space squid army was coming, and nothing would ever be the same again.

ZORVATH SAT AT THE head of the conference table, surrounded by the greatest minds in the galaxy. There was Dr. Vraxxis, the brilliant but slightly unhinged WfRX scientist; Dr. Zara, a renowned expert in genetic engineering; Dr. Thorvath, a master of artificial intelligence; and Admiral Xeridia, a seasoned military strategist.

"Gentlemen, ladies," Zorvath began, his voice commanding attention. "We are here today to discuss the most ambitious project in the history of the WfRX: the creation of a giant space squid army."

CROSSING THE COSMIC HORIZON

Dr. Vraxxis rubbed his hands together in excitement. "Yes, yes, my lord! With the right combination of genetic engineering and artificial intelligence, we can create a squid army that will be unstoppable!"

Dr. Zara nodded in agreement. "I concur, my lord. With advanced genetic engineering, we can enhance the squids' cognitive abilities, making them capable of complex decision-making and strategy."

Dr. Thorvath spoke up next. "And with the integration of artificial intelligence, we can create a neural network that will allow the squids to communicate and coordinate with each other seamlessly."

Admiral Xeridia leaned forward, her eyes narrowing. "But, my lord, have we considered the logistical implications of deploying a giant space squid army? We'll need to develop advanced transportation systems, not to mention strategies for feeding and maintaining these creatures in space."

Zorvath waved his hand dismissively. "Details, details. We will figure it out. The important thing is that we have the vision and the expertise to make this happen."

The room fell silent as the assembled experts pondered the enormity of the task before them. But Zorvath's enthusiasm was infectious, and soon they were all brainstorming and throwing around ideas like crazy.

As the meeting drew to a close, Zorvath stood up, a triumphant smile spreading across his face. "It's settled then. We will create the greatest army the galaxy has ever seen. And with it, we will conquer the stars!"

The room erupted in a chorus of cheers and applause, with Dr. Vraxxis shouting "Squid power!" at the top of his lungs. Zorvath laughed, basking in the admiration of his team.

But as the celebration died down and the experts began to file out of the room, Admiral Xeridia approached Zorvath with a concerned look on her face.

"My lord," she said quietly, "are you certain this is wise? We're talking about creating an army of giant space squids here. What if they get out of control?"

Zorvath's smile faltered for a moment, but then he laughed. "Don't worry, Admiral. I have a plan. And with the greatest minds in the galaxy working for me, I know we can make this happen."

But as Admiral Xeridia walked away, she couldn't shake the feeling that Zorvath's plan was doomed to fail. And that the consequences of failure would be catastrophic.

I watched as Admiral Xeridia walked away, a look of concern etched on her face. I couldn't blame her. The idea of creating an army of giant space squids was, to say the least, unconventional.

As a scientist, I had always been driven by a desire to push the boundaries of what was thought possible. And Zorvath's plan, as crazy as it seemed, was certainly ambitious.

I turned my attention back to the task at hand. I had been tasked with developing the genetic engineering protocols necessary to create the giant space squids. It was a daunting task, but I was confident that I could make it work.

As I delved deeper into my research, I began to realize just how complex this project was going to be. The squids would need to be engineered to survive in the harsh conditions of space, and to be capable of navigating and communicating with each other.

But despite the challenges, I couldn't help but feel a sense of excitement. This was, after all, a chance to make history. To create something that had never been seen before.

I spent the next several hours pouring over my research, making notes and developing a plan of action. As the sun began to set on the space station, I finally felt like I had a handle on the project.

I stood up, stretching my arms over my head. It was going to be a long and difficult road ahead, but I was ready for the challenge.

CROSSING THE COSMIC HORIZON

As I walked out of the laboratory, I was greeted by the sight of Zorvath, standing in the corridor, a look of intense focus on his face.

"Dr. Vraxxis," he said, his voice low and urgent. "I have been thinking. We need to accelerate the timeline for this project. I want to see the first batch of giant space squids within six months."

I felt a surge of alarm at his words. Six months was an impossibly short timeline for a project of this complexity.

"My lord," I said, trying to reason with him. "I understand your enthusiasm, but this is a highly complex project. We can't rush it. We need time to test, to refine, to ensure that the squids are stable and functional."

Zorvath's face darkened, his eyes flashing with anger. "I don't pay you to question my judgment, Dr. Vraxxis," he snarled. "I pay you to make it happen. And I expect results."

I swallowed hard, feeling a chill run down my spine. I knew that I had to tread carefully. Zorvath was not a man to be trifled with.

"Yes, my lord," I said, trying to keep my tone neutral. "I will do my best to accelerate the project."

Zorvath's face relaxed, a cold smile spreading across his face. "I knew I could count on you, Dr. Vraxxis," he said. "Together, we will change the course of history."

I nodded, trying to hide my doubts. But as I walked away, I couldn't shake the feeling that I was being pulled into a nightmare from which I might never awaken.

Dr. Elara Vraxxis stood up, stretching her arms over her head. She had spent the last several hours pouring over her research, making notes and developing a plan of action for the giant space squid project.

As she walked out of the laboratory, she was greeted by the sight of Lord Zorvath, standing in the corridor, a look of intense focus on his face.

"Dr. Vraxxis," Lord Zorvath said, his voice low and urgent. "I have been thinking. We need to accelerate the timeline for this project. I want to see the first batch of giant space squids within six months."

Dr. Vraxxis felt a surge of alarm at his words. "Lord Zorvath, I understand your enthusiasm, but this is a highly complex project," she said. "We can't rush it. We need time to test, to refine, to ensure that the squids are stable and functional."

Lord Zorvath's face darkened, his eyes flashing with anger. "I don't pay you to question my judgment, Dr. Vraxxis," he snarled. "I pay you to make it happen. And I expect results."

Dr. Vraxxis swallowed hard, feeling a chill run down her spine. She knew that she had to tread carefully. Lord Zorvath was not a man to be trifled with.

"Yes, Lord Zorvath," she said, trying to keep her tone neutral. "I will do my best to accelerate the project."

Lord Zorvath's face relaxed, a cold smile spreading across his face. "I knew I could count on you, Dr. Vraxxis," he said. "Together, we will change the course of history."

Dr. Vraxxis nodded, trying to hide her doubts. But as she walked away, she couldn't shake the feeling that she was being pulled into a nightmare from which she might never awaken.

"Dr. Vraxxis," Lord Zorvath called out after her.

"Yes, Lord Zorvath?" she replied, turning back to face him.

"I want you to work closely with Dr. Arcturus Rahl," he said. "He will be assisting you with the genetic engineering aspects of the project."

Dr. Vraxxis nodded, feeling a sense of trepidation. She had heard of Dr. Rahl's unconventional methods and his reputation for being ruthless in his pursuit of scientific progress.

"Yes, Lord Zorvath," she said. "I will work closely with Dr. Rahl to ensure the success of the project."

CROSSING THE COSMIC HORIZON

Lord Zorvath nodded, a look of satisfaction on his face. "I knew I could count on you, Dr. Vraxxis," he said. "Now, go. We have a galaxy to conquer."

Dr. Vraxxis made her way to the laboratory where Dr. Rahl was waiting for her. She had heard rumors about his unorthodox methods and his willingness to push the boundaries of ethics in the pursuit of scientific progress.

As she entered the laboratory, she saw Dr. Rahl standing in front of a large tank filled with a murky liquid. He was a tall, thin man with a gaunt face and sunken eyes. He looked up as Dr. Vraxxis approached.

"Ah, Dr. Vraxxis," he said, his voice dripping with sarcasm. "I've been expecting you. Lord Zorvath has told me great things about your work."

Dr. Vraxxis felt a shiver run down her spine as Dr. Rahl's eyes seemed to bore into her soul. She tried to compose herself, reminding herself that she was a professional.

"Dr. Rahl," she said, trying to keep her tone neutral. "I've been assigned to work with you on the giant space squid project. I understand that you'll be assisting me with the genetic engineering aspects of the project."

Dr. Rahl nodded, a cold smile spreading across his face. "Yes, Dr. Vraxxis. I'll be helping you to create the most advanced, the most powerful, and the most terrifying creatures the galaxy has ever seen."

Dr. Vraxxis felt a sense of unease as Dr. Rahl's eyes seemed to gleam with excitement. She tried to push aside her doubts, reminding herself that she was working for the greater good.

But as she looked into Dr. Rahl's eyes, she couldn't shake the feeling that she was making a terrible mistake.

"So, Dr. Rahl," she said, trying to keep her tone light. "Where do we begin?"

Dr. Rahl's smile grew wider, his eyes glinting with malevolence. "We begin with the basics, Dr. Vraxxis," he said. "We'll start by creating a new species of squid, one that's capable of surviving in the harsh conditions of space."

Dr. Vraxxis nodded, taking notes as Dr. Rahl began to explain his plan. But as she listened, she couldn't shake the feeling that they were playing with forces beyond their control.

And that the consequences of their actions would be catastrophic.

Dr. Rahl's notes were scattered across the laboratory table, filled with diagrams and equations that seemed to dance across the page. Dr. Vraxxis leaned in, her eyes scanning the notes as Dr. Rahl began to explain his plan.

"The species we're creating will be known as Architeuthis Zorvathii," Dr. Rahl said, his voice dripping with excitement. "It will be a massive creature, with a mantle length of up to 100 meters and a mass of several thousand tons."

Dr. Vraxxis's eyes widened as she scanned the notes. "That's enormous," she said. "How do you plan to achieve that level of growth?"

Dr. Rahl smiled, his eyes glinting with pride. "We'll be using a combination of genetic engineering and advanced biomaterials to create a creature that's capable of surviving in the harsh conditions of space."

Dr. Vraxxis nodded, her eyes scanning the notes. "I see you've included a number of adaptations to allow the creature to survive in microgravity," she said. "The addition of statocysts to maintain balance and orientation is a nice touch."

Dr. Rahl nodded, his smile growing wider. "Yes, and we'll also be incorporating a number of other adaptations to allow the creature to thrive in space. The ability to photosynthesize, for example, will allow it to generate energy from the limited sunlight available in space."

Dr. Vraxxis's eyes widened as she scanned the notes. "You're planning to give it a chloroplast-based photosynthetic system?" she asked.

CROSSING THE COSMIC HORIZON

Dr. Rahl nodded. "Yes, we'll be using a combination of chloroplasts and advanced nanotechnology to create a system that's capable of generating energy from even the limited sunlight available in space."

Dr. Vraxxis shook her head, her eyes scanning the notes in amazement. "This is incredible," she said. "You're pushing the boundaries of what's thought possible with genetic engineering and biomaterials."

Dr. Rahl smiled, his eyes glinting with pride. "We're not just pushing the boundaries, Dr. Vraxxis," he said. "We're redefining them."

As Dr. Vraxxis continued to scan the notes, she came across a section detailing the creature's propulsion system. "You're planning to use a combination of jet propulsion and bio-luminescence to propel the creature through space?" she asked, her eyes widening in amazement.

Dr. Rahl nodded, his smile growing wider. "Yes, we'll be using a specialized form of jet propulsion that utilizes the creature's own bodily fluids to generate thrust. And the bio-luminescence will not only provide additional propulsion, but also serve as a means of communication and defense."

Dr. Vraxxis shook her head, her eyes scanning the notes in awe. "This is incredible," she said. "You're creating a creature that's not only capable of surviving in space, but also of thriving in it."

Dr. Rahl nodded, his eyes glinting with pride. "Yes, we're pushing the boundaries of what's thought possible with genetic engineering and biomaterials. And with the Architeuthis Zorvathii, we'll be creating a creature that's truly one of a kind."

As Dr. Vraxxis continued to scan the notes, she came across a section detailing the creature's cognitive abilities. "You're planning to give the creature a advanced cognitive architecture?" she asked, her eyes widening in surprise.

Dr. Rahl nodded, his smile growing wider. "Yes, we'll be using a combination of advanced neural networks and artificial intelligence to create a creature that's capable of complex decision-making and problem-solving."

Dr. Vraxxis shook her head, her eyes scanning the notes in awe. "This is incredible," she said. "You're creating a creature that's not only capable of surviving in space, but also of thinking and adapting like a sentient being."

Dr. Rahl nodded, his eyes glinting with pride. "Yes, we're pushing the boundaries of what's thought possible with genetic engineering and biomaterials. And with the Architeuthis Zorvathii, we'll be creating a creature that's truly one of a kind."

DR. RAHL'S EYES LIT up with excitement as he leaned forward, his voice taking on a conspiratorial tone. "Ah, Dr. Vraxxis, you're thinking like a true visionary. Giving the Architeuthis Zorvathii consciousness and free will would indeed be a game-changer. Just imagine it: an army of sentient, intelligent, and loyal creatures, fighting on our behalf with a ferocity and cunning that would be unmatched in the galaxy."

Dr. Vraxxis's eyes widened as she considered the implications. "But, Dr. Rahl, are you sure that's possible? I mean, we're talking about creating a sentient being here. That's a huge responsibility."

Dr. Rahl waved his hand dismissively. "Pah, responsibility? Ha! We're scientists, Dr. Vraxxis. We're pushing the boundaries of what's possible. And if that means creating a sentient being, then so be it. We'll just have to make sure that we can control them, of course."

Dr. Vraxxis's eyes narrowed. "Control them? Dr. Rahl, I thought we were talking about giving them free will."

Dr. Rahl's smile grew wider. "Ah, yes, yes, of course. Free will. But, you see, Dr. Vraxxis, free will is just a myth. We'll just have to make sure that we program them with the right... let's call them 'motivations'. Yes, that's it. Motivations. We'll make sure that they're loyal only to us, and that they'll fight to the death to protect our interests."

CROSSING THE COSMIC HORIZON

Dr. Vraxxis's face went pale. "Dr. Rahl, I don't know if I'm comfortable with this. We're talking about creating sentient beings here. Beings with thoughts and feelings and desires. We can't just program them like machines."

Dr. Rahl's expression turned cold. "Dr. Vraxxis, I thought you were a scientist. I thought you were committed to pushing the boundaries of what's possible. But it seems that you're just a sentimental fool. Fine. If you're not willing to do what it takes to achieve greatness, then perhaps you're not the right person for this project."

Dr. Vraxxis's eyes flashed with anger. "I'm not a sentimental fool, Dr. Rahl. I'm a scientist who cares about the implications of what we're doing. And I'm not going to stand by and watch you create sentient beings just to use them as cannon fodder."

Dr. Rahl's smile grew wider. "Ah, Dr. Vraxxis. You're so predictable. I knew you'd react this way. But it's too late now. The project is already underway. And soon, we'll have an army of sentient, intelligent, and loyal creatures at our disposal. Creatures that will fight to the death to protect our interests."

Dr. Vraxxis's eyes went wide with horror. "What have you done, Dr. Rahl?" she whispered.

Dr. Rahl's smile grew even wider as he gestured to Dr. Vraxxis to follow him. "Come, Dr. Vraxxis. It's time to present our discovery to Lord Zorvath."

Dr. Vraxxis hesitated for a moment, her mind racing with the implications of what Dr. Rahl had just revealed. But she knew that she had to see this through, no matter how unsettling it was.

She followed Dr. Rahl to the throne room, where Lord Zorvath was waiting for them. He was seated on his throne, his eyes fixed intently on the two scientists.

"Ah, Dr. Rahl, Dr. Vraxxis," he said, his voice dripping with anticipation. "I trust you have made progress on the Architeuthis Zorvathii project?"

Dr. Rahl bowed low, a smug look on his face. "Yes, my lord. We have made a breakthrough. We have successfully created a sentient, intelligent, and loyal creature that will fight to the death to protect our interests."

Lord Zorvath's eyes lit up with excitement. "Ah, excellent! I knew that with the right team, we could achieve greatness. Tell me, Dr. Rahl, what is the current status of the creature?"

Dr. Rahl smiled, clearly pleased with himself. "The creature is currently in the larval stage, my lord. But we expect it to mature rapidly, and we anticipate that it will be ready for deployment within a few months."

Lord Zorvath nodded, a look of satisfaction on his face. "Excellent. I want to see the creature for myself. Arrange for me to visit the laboratory immediately."

Dr. Rahl bowed low. "Yes, my lord. I will arrange for you to visit the laboratory at once."

As Dr. Rahl and Dr. Vraxxis left the throne room, Dr. Vraxxis couldn't help but feel a sense of unease. She knew that she had to find a way to stop this project, before it was too late.

But for now, she had to play along, and pretend that she was excited about the prospect of creating an army of sentient, intelligent, and loyal creatures.

As they walked to the laboratory, Dr. Rahl turned to her with a smug look on his face. "You see, Dr. Vraxxis, I told you that we could do it. We're on the brink of a new era in genetic engineering, and we're going to change the course of history."

Dr. Vraxxis forced a smile onto her face. "Yes, Dr. Rahl. It's certainly an exciting time to be a scientist."

But as she looked at Dr. Rahl, she couldn't help but feel a sense of disgust. She knew that she had to find a way to stop him, before he could carry out his twisted plans.

CROSSING THE COSMIC HORIZON

As they arrived at the laboratory, Dr. Vraxxis couldn't help but feel a sense of unease. She knew that she was about to witness something that would change the course of history, but she was also deeply concerned about the ethics of the project.

Dr. Rahl led them to a large tank in the center of the laboratory, where a massive, tentacled creature was floating in the water. Dr. Vraxxis gasped in amazement as she realized the sheer size of the creature.

"Behold, my lord," Dr. Rahl said, bowing low to Lord Zorvath. "The Architeuthis Zorvathii, the most advanced, sentient, and intelligent creature in the galaxy."

Lord Zorvath's eyes widened in amazement as he approached the tank. "It's magnificent," he breathed. "The perfect creature to serve as our loyal soldiers."

Dr. Vraxxis felt a shiver run down her spine as she watched Lord Zorvath's reaction. She knew that she had to find a way to stop this project, before it was too late.

But as she looked at the creature, she felt a pang of sadness. It was a magnificent being, with a level of intelligence and sentience that was unmatched in the galaxy. And yet, it was being created solely for the purpose of serving as a soldier, a tool of war.

Dr. Vraxxis knew that she had to act, and fast. She couldn't let this creature be used for such nefarious purposes. She had to find a way to stop the project, no matter the cost.

As Lord Zorvath and Dr. Rahl continued to marvel at the creature, Dr. Vraxxis slipped away, determined to find a way to sabotage the project and free the Architeuthis Zorvathii from its fate as a soldier.

As Dr. Vraxxis slipped away, Dr. Rahl's thoughts turned to the next phase of the project. He was excited to see the Architeuthis Zorvathii in action, to see how it would perform in combat.

"But first, I need to make sure that it's loyal only to us," Dr. Rahl thought to himself. "I'll need to program it with a strong sense of loyalty and obedience. And perhaps a few... safeguards, just in case it gets out of hand."

Dr. Rahl's thoughts turned to the possibilities of what the Architeuthis Zorvathii could do. "With an army of these creatures at our disposal, we'll be unstoppable," he thought. "We'll be able to conquer the entire galaxy, and no one will be able to stand in our way."

As Dr. Rahl's thoughts continued to spin with excitement and ambition, he didn't notice Dr. Vraxxis watching him from across the room. She had slipped back into the laboratory, determined to learn more about Dr. Rahl's plans and to find a way to stop him.

Dr. Vraxxis's eyes narrowed as she watched Dr. Rahl. She could see the excitement and ambition in his eyes, and she knew that she had to be careful. She couldn't let Dr. Rahl suspect that she was onto him, or he would stop at nothing to silence her.

As Dr. Vraxxis continued to watch Dr. Rahl, she began to piece together the full extent of his plan. She realized that he intended to use the Architeuthis Zorvathii not just as soldiers, but as a means of controlling the entire galaxy.

Dr. Vraxxis's heart sank as she realized the true extent of Dr. Rahl's ambition. She knew that she had to act fast, to stop Dr. Rahl before it was too late. But as she turned to leave, she was confronted by Dr. Rahl himself.

"Ah, Dr. Vraxxis," Dr. Rahl said, his eyes glinting with suspicion. "I see you're interested in the Architeuthis Zorvathii. Perhaps you'd like to take a closer look?"

Dr. Vraxxis's heart skipped a beat as she realized that Dr. Rahl was onto her. She knew that she had to think fast, to come up with a convincing excuse for why she was snooping around the laboratory.

"I was just... uh... looking for some data on the creature's cognitive abilities," Dr. Vraxxis stammered.

Dr. Rahl's eyes narrowed. "I see," he said. "Well, in that case, perhaps I can show you some of our latest research."

CROSSING THE COSMIC HORIZON

Dr. Vraxxis's heart sank as Dr. Rahl led her deeper into the laboratory. She knew that she was in grave danger, and that she had to think fast if she was going to get out of this situation alive.

Dr. Rahl led Dr. Vraxxis to a large console in the center of the laboratory, where a holographic display flickered with data.

"Ah, yes," Dr. Rahl said, gesturing to the display. "As you can see, we've made significant breakthroughs in the creature's cognitive abilities. We've been able to program it with a sophisticated neural network, allowing it to learn and adapt at an exponential rate."

Dr. Vraxxis's eyes widened as she scanned the data. "This is incredible," she said. "But how do you plan to control it? I mean, with a creature this intelligent and adaptable, there's a risk that it could become uncontrollable."

Dr. Rahl chuckled. "Ah, Dr. Vraxxis, you're thinking like a traditional scientist. But we're not just creating a creature, we're creating a tool. A tool that will be loyal only to us, and will do our bidding without question."

Dr. Vraxxis's eyes narrowed. "And how do you plan to ensure that loyalty?" she asked.

Dr. Rahl smiled. "Ah, that's the beauty of it. We've developed a new form of neural programming that allows us to implant a set of core directives deep within the creature's brain. Directives that will override any other impulse or desire the creature may have."

Dr. Vraxxis's face went pale. "You're talking about creating a slave," she said. "A creature that will be forced to do your bidding without any free will of its own."

Dr. Rahl shrugged. "Call it what you will, Dr. Vraxxis. The fact remains that we're creating a tool that will allow us to achieve our goals. And if that means sacrificing a little bit of free will, then so be it."

Dr. Vraxxis's eyes flashed with anger. "You're playing God, Dr. Rahl," she said. "And you're going to regret it."

Dr. Rahl laughed. "I'm not playing God, Dr. Vraxxis," he said. "I'm just pushing the boundaries of what's possible. And if you're not willing to do the same, then perhaps you're not the right person for this project."

Dr. Vraxxis's face went cold. "I'll do what it takes to stop you, Dr. Rahl," she said. "Even if it means sacrificing my own career."

Dr. Rahl's smile grew wider. "I'm shaking in my boots, Dr. Vraxxis," he said. "But I think you'll find that you're no match for me. I have the backing of Lord Zorvath, and I will stop at nothing to achieve my goals."

Dr. Vraxxis's eyes narrowed. "We'll see about that," she said.

DR. RAHL'S SMILE FALTERED for a moment, and Dr. Vraxxis saw a flash of anger in his eyes. But then, his expression smoothed out, and he chuckled.

"I'm looking forward to seeing you try, Dr. Vraxxis," he said. "But for now, I think it's time for you to leave. You've seen enough for one day."

Dr. Vraxxis nodded, her mind racing with thoughts of how she could stop Dr. Rahl and his sinister plans. She turned to leave, but as she reached the door, she heard Dr. Rahl's voice behind her.

"Dr. Vraxxis," he said.

She turned to see him standing in the center of the room, a small, cruel smile playing on his lips.

"Yes?" she asked.

"I almost forgot," Dr. Rahl said. "Lord Zorvath has requested your presence at a meeting tomorrow morning. I'm sure you'll want to be there."

Dr. Vraxxis's heart sank. She had a feeling that she was in grave danger, and that Dr. Rahl and Lord Zorvath were planning something that would put her at the center of their sinister plans.

CROSSING THE COSMIC HORIZON

"I'll be there," she said, trying to keep her voice steady.

Dr. Rahl nodded, his smile growing wider. "I'm looking forward to it," he said.

Dr. Vraxxis turned and left the laboratory, her mind racing with thoughts of how she could escape the clutches of Dr. Rahl and Lord Zorvath. She knew that she had to act fast, before it was too late.

As she walked back to her quarters, she couldn't shake the feeling that she was being watched. She glanced over her shoulder, but saw nothing out of the ordinary.

Still, the feeling persisted. Dr. Vraxxis quickened her pace, her heart pounding in her chest. She knew that she had to be careful, that one misstep could mean disaster.

She reached her quarters and locked the door behind her, feeling a sense of relief wash over her. But as she turned to enter her living area, she saw something that made her blood run cold.

On her console, a message was flashing, addressed to her. It was from an unknown sender, and all it said was:

"We know what you're planning. Meet us in the east wing at midnight if you want to live."

Dr. Vraxxis's heart was racing as she stared at the message. Who could have sent it? And what did they want from her?

She knew that she had to be careful, that this could be a trap. But she also knew that she couldn't ignore the message. She had to know what was going on, and who was behind it.

With a sense of trepidation, Dr. Vraxxis made her way to the east wing at midnight, wondering what lay ahead.

AS DR. VRAXXIS MADE her way to the east wing, she couldn't shake the feeling that she was being watched. She glanced over her shoulder, but saw nothing out of the ordinary. Still, the feeling persisted.

She arrived at the east wing, her heart pounding in her chest. The hallway was dimly lit, and the air was thick with an eerie silence. Dr. Vraxxis's skin crawled as she made her way down the hallway, her eyes scanning the shadows for any sign of movement.

Suddenly, a figure emerged from the darkness. Dr. Vraxxis's heart skipped a beat as she saw that it was a woman, dressed in a black jumpsuit and carrying a small bag slung over her shoulder.

"Who are you?" Dr. Vraxxis demanded, trying to keep her voice steady.

"My name is not important," the woman replied, her voice low and husky. "What's important is that I have information that you need to know."

Dr. Vraxxis's eyes narrowed. "What kind of information?"

The woman smiled, a small, enigmatic smile. "Information about Dr. Rahl's true intentions," she said. "Information about the Architeuthis Zorvathii, and what it's really capable of."

Dr. Vraxxis's heart was racing now. She knew that she had to hear what this woman had to say.

"Tell me," she said, her voice barely above a whisper.

The woman nodded, and began to speak in a low, urgent tone. "Dr. Rahl's plan is not just to create a new species of sentient being," she said. "It's to use that species to gain control over the entire galaxy."

Dr. Vraxxis's eyes widened in horror. "How?" she demanded.

The woman smiled again, her eyes glinting with a fierce determination. "That's what I'm here to tell you," she said. "But first, we need to get out of here. We're not safe."

Dr. Vraxxis nodded, her mind racing with the implications of what she had just heard. She knew that she had to trust this woman, at least for now.

Together, the two women made their way through the dark and deserted corridors of the laboratory, their hearts pounding with anticipation and fear. They knew that they were taking a huge risk, but they also knew that they had no choice.

As they walked, the woman turned to Dr. Vraxxis and smiled. "My name is Maya, by the way," she said.

Dr. Vraxxis smiled back, feeling a sense of gratitude and relief. "I'm Dr. Vraxxis," she said. "And I'm glad to have you on my side, Maya."

Maya nodded, her eyes glinting with determination. "We're in this together now, Dr. Vraxxis," she said. "And we're going to bring down Dr. Rahl and his sinister plans, no matter what it takes."

As they walked, Maya led Dr. Vraxxis to a small, unassuming door hidden behind a row of crates. Maya produced a small keycard and swiped it through the lock, causing the door to slide open with a soft hiss.

"Welcome to our little hideout," Maya said, gesturing for Dr. Vraxxis to enter.

Dr. Vraxxis stepped through the doorway and found herself in a small, cramped room filled with computer terminals and various pieces of equipment. Maya followed close behind, closing the door and locking it behind them.

"Okay, we should be safe here," Maya said, turning to face Dr. Vraxxis. "This room is shielded from the rest of the lab, and I've taken steps to ensure that we can't be monitored or tracked."

Dr. Vraxxis nodded, feeling a sense of relief wash over her. She was finally safe, at least for the moment.

"Okay, Maya," she said, turning to face the other woman. "Tell me more about Dr. Rahl's plans. What exactly is he trying to do?"

Maya's expression turned grim. "Dr. Rahl's plan is to use the Architeuthis Zorvathii to gain control over the entire galaxy," she said. "He's been working on a way to harness the creature's power and use it to manipulate the minds of others. He wants to create an army of mindless drones that will do his bidding without question."

Dr. Vraxxis's eyes widened in horror. "That's monstrous," she said. "We can't let him do it."

Maya nodded, her expression determined. "I agree," she said. "But we need to be careful. Dr. Rahl has a lot of power and influence, and he won't hesitate to use it to crush anyone who gets in his way."

Dr. Vraxxis nodded, feeling a sense of determination wash over her. She was ready to take on Dr. Rahl and his sinister plans, no matter the cost.

"Okay, Maya," she said. "Let's get to work. We have a lot to do if we're going to stop Dr. Rahl and save the galaxy."

Maya smiled, a fierce glint in her eye. "I'm with you, Dr. Vraxxis," she said. "Let's do this."

AS THEY BEGAN TO BRAINSTORM their plan, Dr. Vraxxis's mind was racing with thoughts of the Architeuthis Zorvathii and the potential consequences of Dr. Rahl's plan.

"We need to get to the creature before Dr. Rahl does," Dr. Vraxxis said, her eyes locked on Maya's. "We need to stop him before he can harness its power."

Maya nodded, her expression grim. "I agree," she said. "But we need to be careful. Dr. Rahl has a lot of security measures in place to protect the creature. We'll need to be clever if we're going to get past them."

Dr. Vraxxis nodded, her mind already racing with ideas. "I think I can help with that," she said. "I've been studying the lab's security systems, and I think I can find a way to disable them long enough for us to get to the creature."

Maya's eyes lit up with excitement. "That's perfect," she said. "With your knowledge of the security systems and my knowledge of the lab's layout, I think we can pull this off."

As they continued to brainstorm, Dr. Vraxxis couldn't help but feel a sense of excitement and purpose. She was finally doing something to stop Dr. Rahl and his sinister plans, and she was determined to see it through.

But as they were about to put their plan into action, they heard a noise coming from outside the room. It sounded like footsteps, heavy and deliberate.

Maya's eyes locked on Dr. Vraxxis's, and she mouthed a single word: "Run."

Dr. Vraxxis didn't need to be told twice. She quickly grabbed her bag and followed Maya out of the room, just as the door burst open and a group of heavily armed guards stormed in.

"Dr. Vraxxis, you're coming with us," one of the guards growled, his eyes fixed on her.

Dr. Vraxxis stood tall, her heart pounding in her chest. "I'm not going anywhere," she said, her voice firm.

But before she could say anything else, Maya grabbed her arm and pulled her away, leading her down a narrow corridor and into the depths of the lab.

As they ran, Dr. Vraxxis could hear the guards shouting behind them, their footsteps echoing off the walls. She knew that they had to move fast if they were going to escape.

But where were they going? And what would they find when they got there?

As they ran, Maya led Dr. Vraxxis through a maze of corridors and stairways, dodging security cameras and avoiding detection. They finally reached a small door hidden behind a ventilation shaft, and Maya produced a keycard to unlock it.

"Where are we going?" Dr. Vraxxis asked, panting with exertion.

"We're going to the one place in the lab where we can be sure of finding the truth," Maya replied, her eyes glinting with determination. "The central database."

Dr. Vraxxis's eyes widened in surprise. "The central database?" she repeated. "But that's heavily guarded. How do you plan to get us in?"

Maya smiled, a mischievous glint in her eye. "Leave that to me," she said. "I've been working on a little plan to get us past the guards. Follow me."

Maya led Dr. Vraxxis through a narrow maintenance tunnel, dodging pipes and ductwork as they made their way deeper into the lab. They finally emerged into a large, dimly lit room filled with row upon row of computer terminals and data storage units.

"The central database," Maya said, her voice barely above a whisper. "This is where all the lab's most sensitive information is stored. If we can get into the system, we should be able to find out what Dr. Rahl is really planning."

Dr. Vraxxis's eyes widened as she gazed around the room. "But how do we get into the system?" she asked. "I'm sure it's heavily encrypted."

Maya smiled again, her eyes glinting with confidence. "Leave that to me," she said. "I've been working on a little something to help us get past the security measures. Watch this."

Maya pulled out a small device from her pocket and attached it to one of the computer terminals. She typed in a few quick commands, and the terminal sprang to life, displaying a complex pattern of code and data.

"What is that?" Dr. Vraxxis asked, her eyes widening in amazement.

"It's a backdoor program I've been working on," Maya replied, her fingers flying across the keyboard. "It should give us access to the entire system, including all the classified files and research data."

Dr. Vraxxis's eyes widened as she watched Maya work her magic on the computer terminal. She had never seen anyone hack into a system so quickly and easily before.

As they worked, Dr. Vraxxis couldn't help but feel a sense of excitement and anticipation. They were getting close to the truth, and she could feel it.

CROSSING THE COSMIC HORIZON

But as they delved deeper into the system, they began to uncover some disturbing secrets. Secrets that would change everything they thought they knew about the lab and its true purpose.

"What's this?" Dr. Vraxxis asked, her voice barely above a whisper. "A secret project codenamed 'Erebus'?"

Maya's eyes locked on hers, a look of grave concern etched on her face. "I don't know what it is," she said, "but I think we need to find out."

As they continued to dig deeper into the system, they uncovered more and more disturbing secrets. They found evidence of secret experiments, hidden laboratories, and mysterious projects with codenames like "Erebus" and "Nemesis".

Dr. Vraxxis's eyes widened as she read through the files, her mind reeling with the implications. "This is insane," she whispered. "They're playing with forces they don't even begin to understand."

Maya nodded, her expression grim. "I know," she said. "I've been trying to tell you, but you wouldn't listen."

Dr. Vraxxis turned to her, a look of shock on her face. "You knew about this?" she asked.

Maya nodded. "I've been investigating Dr. Rahl's activities for months," she said. "I knew he was up to something, but I had no idea it was this bad."

Dr. Vraxxis's eyes narrowed. "Why didn't you tell me?" she asked.

Maya shrugged. "I didn't think you'd believe me," she said. "And even if you did, I wasn't sure you'd be willing to take the risks necessary to stop Dr. Rahl."

Dr. Vraxxis's expression softened. "I'm sorry," she said. "I should have listened to you sooner."

Maya smiled, a small, sad smile. "It's not your fault," she said. "We're both just pawns in Dr. Rahl's game. But we can change that. We can take control of our own destiny, and stop Dr. Rahl before it's too late."

Dr. Vraxxis nodded, a sense of determination rising up within her. "Let's do it," she said. "Let's take down Dr. Rahl and his sinister plans once and for all."

Maya grinned, a fierce glint in her eye. "It's time to take back control," she said. "Let's do this."

Together, the two women set out on their mission to stop Dr. Rahl and his sinister plans. They knew it wouldn't be easy, but they were determined to succeed.

As they made their way through the lab, avoiding security guards and dodging danger at every turn, Dr. Vraxxis couldn't help but feel a sense of excitement and anticipation. They were on a mission to save the world, and she was proud to be a part of it.

But as they approached the heart of the lab, they were met with a shocking sight. Dr. Rahl stood in front of them, a smug look on his face.

"Welcome, Dr. Vraxxis," he said. "I've been expecting you. You're just in time to witness the culmination of my life's work."

Dr. Vraxxis's eyes narrowed. "What are you talking about?" she asked.

Dr. Rahl smiled. "Why, the birth of the Architeuthis Zorvathii, of course," he said. "The creature is ready to be unleashed upon the world. And you, Dr. Vraxxis, are going to be the one to do it."

Dr. Rahl's eyes gleamed with excitement as he began to explain the details of Project Nemesis. "You see, Dr. Vraxxis, Project Nemesis is the codename for a top-secret research initiative that aims to create a new breed of super-soldiers using advanced genetic engineering and cybernetic enhancements."

Dr. Vraxxis's eyes widened in horror as she listened to Dr. Rahl's explanation. "You're talking about creating a new breed of humans," she said. "Humans that are genetically engineered to be stronger, faster, and more agile than regular humans."

Dr. Rahl nodded enthusiastically. "That's right," he said. "And not only that, but we're also planning to implant them with advanced cybernetic enhancements that will give them enhanced strength, agility, and reflexes. We're talking about creating a new breed of super-soldiers that will be capable of carrying out missions that would be impossible for regular humans."

Dr. Vraxxis's face went pale as she listened to Dr. Rahl's explanation. "This is monstrous," she said. "You're talking about creating a new breed of humans that will be nothing more than mindless drones, programmed to carry out your every command."

Dr. Rahl's expression turned cold. "You're just not seeing the bigger picture, Dr. Vraxxis," he said. "Project Nemesis is not just about creating a new breed of super-soldiers. It's about creating a new breed of humans that will be capable of surviving in a world that is rapidly becoming more and more hostile."

Dr. Vraxxis's eyes narrowed. "What do you mean by 'a world that is rapidly becoming more and more hostile'?" she asked.

Dr. Rahl's expression turned grim. "I'm talking about the fact that the world is facing a number of catastrophic threats, from climate change to nuclear war," he said. "And in order to survive in a world like that, humans are going to need to be stronger, faster, and more agile than they are now. That's where Project Nemesis comes in."

Dr. Vraxxis's face went pale as she listened to Dr. Rahl's explanation. She knew that he was right, that the world was facing a number of catastrophic threats. But she also knew that creating a new breed of super-soldiers was not the answer.

"We can't just create a new breed of humans and expect them to solve all our problems," she said. "We need to address the root causes of the problems we're facing, not just try to create a new breed of humans that can survive in a hostile world."

Dr. Rahl's expression turned cold. "You're just not seeing the bigger picture, Dr. Vraxxis," he said. "Project Nemesis is not just about creating a new breed of super-soldiers. It's about creating a new breed of humans that will be capable of surviving in a world that is rapidly becoming more and more hostile. And if you're not willing to see that, then perhaps you're not the right person for this project."

Dr. Vraxxis's eyes narrowed. "I'm not going to let you create a new breed of super-soldiers without a fight," she said. "I'm going to do everything in my power to stop you."

Dr. Rahl's expression turned cold. "We'll see about that," he said.

Dr. Rahl's eyes seemed to bore into Dr. Vraxxis's soul as he spoke. "You're just one person, Dr. Vraxxis," he said. "You can't stop me. I have the backing of Lord Zorvath, and I have the resources of the entire lab at my disposal. You're no match for me."

Dr. Vraxxis stood tall, her eyes flashing with defiance. "I may not be able to stop you alone," she said. "But I'm not alone. I have Maya, and I have the evidence we've uncovered. We'll take you down, Dr. Rahl. Mark my words."

Dr. Rahl's expression turned red with rage. "You'll never leave this lab alive," he spat. "Guards! Take Dr. Vraxxis and Maya into custody. Throw them in the holding cells until I can deal with them personally."

The guards moved to obey, but Dr. Vraxxis and Maya were ready for them. They fought back, using all their skills and training to take down the guards. But they were outnumbered, and it soon became clear that they wouldn't be able to hold out for much longer.

Just when it seemed like all was lost, a loud explosion rocked the lab, causing the lights to flicker and the walls to shake. The guards stumbled, momentarily distracted, and Dr. Vraxxis and Maya took advantage of the opportunity to make their escape.

They ran as fast as they could, dodging debris and leaping over obstacles. They didn't dare look back, fearing what they might see. But they knew they had to keep moving, no matter what.

Finally, they reached the safety of the lab's exit. They burst through the doors, gasping for air, and found themselves in a deserted corridor.

They didn't know where they were, or where they were going. But they knew they had to keep moving.

As they ran, the sound of alarms and explosions grew fainter. They knew they had left the lab behind, and were now in the unknown. But they were together, and they were free. And that was all that mattered.

But as they turned a corner, they were confronted with a shocking sight. A group of heavily armed soldiers, clad in black armor and masks, stood blocking their path. And at their center, a figure in a long, black coat stood watching them, a cold, calculating gaze in his eyes.

"Welcome, Dr. Vraxxis and Maya," the figure said, his voice dripping with malice. "I've been expecting you. My name is Commander Thraxys, and I'm here to take you into custody."

Dr. Vraxxis's eyes narrowed. "You're not going to take us anywhere," she said, her voice firm. "We're not going to let you."

Commander Thraxys smiled, a cold, cruel smile. "We'll see about that," he said.

AS COMMANDER THRAXYS spoke, his soldiers moved to surround Dr. Vraxxis and Maya, their guns trained on the two women. Dr. Vraxxis knew they were outnumbered and outgunned, but she refused to give up.

"We're not going down without a fight," she said, her eyes flashing with defiance.

Commander Thraxys chuckled. "I'm shaking in my boots," he said. "But let's not make this any harder than it has to be. Surrender now, and we might let you live."

Dr. Vraxxis snorted. "You think we're just going to surrender? After everything we've been through?"

Commander Thraxys shrugged. "Suit yourselves," he said. "But don't say I didn't warn you."

With that, he nodded to his soldiers, and they moved in to take Dr. Vraxxis and Maya into custody. But the two women were not going to go down without a fight.

Dr. Vraxxis used her knowledge of the lab's layout to her advantage, leading the soldiers on a wild goose chase through the corridors. Maya, meanwhile, used her agility and quick thinking to take down several of the soldiers, using her knowledge of hand-to-hand combat to overpower them.

Despite being outnumbered, the two women managed to hold their own against the soldiers, using every trick in the book to stay one step ahead. But Commander Thraxys was not a man to be underestimated, and he soon called in reinforcements to help take down Dr. Vraxxis and Maya.

As the battle raged on, Dr. Vraxxis and Maya found themselves surrounded by more and more soldiers, their guns trained on the two women. It seemed like all was lost, and that they would soon be taken into custody.

But just as all hope seemed lost, a loud explosion rocked the corridor, sending soldiers flying and causing chaos. Dr. Vraxxis and Maya took advantage of the distraction to make a break for it, running as fast as they could through the smoke-filled corridors.

As they ran, they could hear the sound of gunfire and explosions behind them, and they knew that they were not out of danger yet. But they refused to give up, using every ounce of strength and determination they possessed to keep going.

Finally, after what seemed like an eternity, they saw a glimmer of light up ahead. They burst through the door and found themselves in a deserted alleyway, the cool night air a welcome relief after the chaos of the lab.

Dr. Vraxxis and Maya looked at each other, their eyes shining with exhaustion and relief. They knew they still had a long way to go, but for now, they had made it out of the lab alive.

CROSSING THE COSMIC HORIZON

As they caught their breath, Dr. Vraxxis turned to Maya and asked, "What's our next move?"

Maya grinned, her eyes sparkling with determination. "We take down Dr. Rahl and his operation, once and for all."

Dr. Vraxxis nodded, a fierce glint in her eye. "Let's do it."

As they made their way through the alleyway, they could hear the sound of footsteps echoing off the walls. Dr. Vraxxis and Maya exchanged a look, and without a word, they knew they were in for a fight.

The first soldier emerged from the shadows, his gun raised and trained on Dr. Vraxxis. But before he could fire, Maya sprang into action, her agility and quick reflexes allowing her to dodge the soldier's attack. She countered with a swift kick to the soldier's stomach, sending him crashing to the ground.

Dr. Vraxxis, meanwhile, had taken down another soldier with a perfectly aimed punch to the jaw. She followed up with a series of rapid-fire punches, each one landing with precision and power.

The soldiers, however, were not easily deterred. They regrouped and launched a fierce counterattack, their guns blazing as they tried to take down Dr. Vraxxis and Maya.

But the two women were more than a match for the soldiers. They dodged and weaved, avoiding the hail of bullets as they launched a series of devastating counterattacks.

Maya took down a soldier with a perfectly executed roundhouse kick, while Dr. Vraxxis used her knowledge of hand-to-hand combat to take down another soldier with a series of swift and precise punches.

As the battle raged on, the alleyway became a scene of utter chaos. Soldiers were scattered everywhere, some of them lying motionless on the ground, while others stumbled around, clutching their wounds.

Dr. Vraxxis and Maya, meanwhile, were a whirlwind of activity, their movements swift and precise as they took down soldier after soldier.

But despite their valiant efforts, they soon found themselves surrounded by an overwhelming number of soldiers. Dr. Vraxxis and Maya were vastly outnumbered, and it seemed like all was lost.

Just when it seemed like the soldiers were about to overpower them, a loud explosion rocked the alleyway, sending soldiers flying and causing chaos. Dr. Vraxxis and Maya took advantage of the distraction to launch a fierce counterattack, using every ounce of strength and determination they possessed to take down the soldiers.

As the battle raged on, the alleyway became a scene of utter devastation. Buildings were reduced to rubble, and the air was thick with the smell of smoke and gunfire.

But despite the chaos and destruction, Dr. Vraxxis and Maya refused to give up. They fought on, their movements swift and precise, as they took down soldier after soldier.

Finally, after what seemed like an eternity, the battle was over. The soldiers lay defeated, and Dr. Vraxxis and Maya stood victorious, their chests heaving with exhaustion.

As they caught their breath, Dr. Vraxxis turned to Maya and asked, "What's our next move?"

Maya grinned, her eyes sparkling with determination. "We take down Dr. Rahl and his operation, once and for all."

Dr. Vraxxis nodded, a fierce glint in her eye. "Let's do it."

Together, the two women set off towards the lab, ready to face whatever dangers lay ahead. They knew it wouldn't be easy, but they were determined to see justice done.

As they walked, they could hear the sound of alarms blaring in the distance. They knew they had to move fast, before Dr. Rahl and his operation could regroup and launch a counterattack.

But Dr. Vraxxis and Maya were not afraid. They were ready for whatever lay ahead, and they were determined to see their mission through to the end.

CROSSING THE COSMIC HORIZON

As they approached the lab, they could see that it was surrounded by a ring of soldiers. Dr. Rahl stood at the entrance, a smug look on his face.

"Welcome, Dr. Vraxxis and Maya," he said, his voice dripping with malice. "I've been expecting you. You're just in time to witness the culmination of my life's work."

Dr. Vraxxis and Maya exchanged a look, and without a word, they knew they were in for the fight of their lives.

As Dr. Rahl spoke, the soldiers surrounding the lab moved to form a semi-circle around Dr. Vraxxis and Maya, trapping them in a ring of steel. Dr. Rahl smiled, clearly enjoying the moment.

"You see, Dr. Vraxxis and Maya," he said, "I've been working on a little project of my own. A project that will change the course of human history forever."

Dr. Vraxxis's eyes narrowed. "What are you talking about, Dr. Rahl?" she asked.

Dr. Rahl chuckled. "Oh, I think you'll see," he said. "You see, I've been working on a machine that can harness the power of the human mind. A machine that can amplify human thought and turn it into reality."

Maya's eyes widened. "You're talking about a mind-control device," she said.

Dr. Rahl nodded. "That's right," he said. "And with this device, I'll be able to control the minds of world leaders, bending them to my will. I'll be able to shape the course of human history, and remake the world in my image."

Dr. Vraxxis's face went white with horror. "You can't be serious," she said.

Dr. Rahl smiled. "Oh, I'm dead serious," he said. "And with the help of my new machine, I'll be able to make my vision a reality."

As Dr. Rahl spoke, the machine behind him began to hum to life. The air around it began to distort and ripple, and a bright light began to emanate from it.

Dr. Vraxxis and Maya exchanged a look, and without a word, they knew they had to act fast. They charged forward, determined to stop Dr. Rahl and his machine before it was too late.

But as they approached the machine, they were met with a shocking sight. The machine was not just a simple device - it was a massive, sprawling complex of wires and circuits, with a glowing crystal at its heart.

And as they watched, the crystal began to glow brighter and brighter, filling the air with an intense, pulsating energy.

Dr. Vraxxis and Maya knew they had to act fast. They charged forward, determined to stop the machine and shatter Dr. Rahl's plans once and for all.

But as they approached the machine, they were met with a shocking sight. Dr. Rahl was not alone. Standing beside him, her eyes glowing with an otherworldly energy, was a figure Dr. Vraxxis and Maya knew all too well.

It was Lord Zorvath's daughter, Lady Arachne. And she was not happy to see Dr. Vraxxis and Maya.

Lady Arachne's eyes narrowed as she gazed at Dr. Vraxxis and Maya. "So, you're the ones who have been causing so much trouble," she said, her voice dripping with venom.

Dr. Vraxxis stood tall, her eyes locked on Lady Arachne. "We're not going to let you and Dr. Rahl carry out your twisted plans," she said.

Lady Arachne laughed, a cold, mirthless sound. "You're no match for us," she said. "We have the power of the Architeuthis Zorvathii on our side. And with this machine, we'll be able to harness that power and use it to control the minds of world leaders."

Maya's eyes widened in horror. "You can't be serious," she said.

CROSSING THE COSMIC HORIZON

Lady Arachne smiled, a cold, calculating smile. "Oh, I'm dead serious," she said. "And with Dr. Rahl's machine, we'll be able to make our vision a reality."

Dr. Vraxxis's eyes locked on the machine, her mind racing with thoughts of how to stop it. She knew that she and Maya had to act fast, before it was too late.

Without hesitation, Dr. Vraxxis charged forward, determined to stop the machine and shatter Dr. Rahl and Lady Arachne's plans once and for all. Maya followed close behind, her eyes fixed on Lady Arachne.

As they approached the machine, Dr. Rahl and Lady Arachne stood their ground, their eyes flashing with determination. "You'll never stop us," Dr. Rahl sneered.

Dr. Vraxxis smiled, a fierce glint in her eye. "We'll see about that," she said.

With a swift motion, Dr. Vraxxis reached out and grabbed a nearby fire extinguisher, using it to smash the machine's control panel. The machine let out a loud whine, its lights flickering wildly as it began to malfunction.

Lady Arachne's eyes widened in rage. "You fools!" she screamed. "You'll pay for this!"

Maya stood tall, her eyes locked on Lady Arachne. "We're not afraid of you," she said.

Lady Arachne's face twisted with anger. "We'll see about that," she said.

With a swift motion, Lady Arachne reached out and grabbed Maya, her eyes flashing with energy. Maya struggled to break free, but Lady Arachne's grip was like a vice.

Dr. Vraxxis's eyes widened in horror. "Maya!" she screamed.

But before she could intervene, Lady Arachne's eyes flashed with energy, and Maya's body went limp. Dr. Vraxxis's eyes widened in horror as she realized that Lady Arachne had used her powers to knock Maya unconscious.

Dr. Vraxxis's face twisted with rage. "You'll pay for this," she said, her voice low and deadly.

Lady Arachne smiled, a cold, calculating smile. "I'm shaking in my boots," she said.

With a swift motion, Dr. Vraxxis charged forward, determined to take down Lady Arachne and shatter Dr. Rahl's plans once and for all. But as she approached Lady Arachne, she was met with a shocking sight.

Lady Arachne's body began to glow with an otherworldly energy, and her eyes flashed with an intense, pulsating power. Dr. Vraxxis's eyes widened in horror as she realized that Lady Arachne was not just a powerful psychic - she was something much, much more.

"Lady Arachne, what's happening to you?" Dr. Rahl asked, his voice filled with concern.

Lady Arachne's eyes flashed with energy. "I am becoming what I was meant to be," she said, her voice low and deadly. "I am becoming the vessel for the Architeuthis Zorvathii."

Dr. Vraxxis's eyes widened in horror. "No," she said. "You can't let that happen."

Lady Arachne's eyes flashed with energy. "It's too late," she said. "The process has already begun. And soon, I will be the most powerful being on the planet."

Dr. Vraxxis knew that she had to act fast. She charged forward, determined to stop Lady Arachne and shatter Dr. Rahl's plans once and for all. But as she approached Lady Arachne, she was met with a shocking sight.

Lady Arachne's body was beginning to transform, her skin turning a deep, pulsing purple. Her eyes were glowing with an intense, otherworldly energy, and her hair was standing on end, as if it was being blown back by an invisible wind.

CROSSING THE COSMIC HORIZON

Dr. Vraxxis's eyes widened in horror. "What's happening to you?" she asked.

Lady

Lady Arachne's voice was no longer human, but a deep, rumbling growl. "I am becoming the vessel," she said. "The Architeuthis Zorvathii is awakening within me."

Dr. Vraxxis took a step back, her eyes fixed on Lady Arachne's transforming body. She knew that she had to act fast, before Lady Arachne was completely consumed by the alien entity.

With a swift motion, Dr. Vraxxis reached out and grabbed a nearby fire extinguisher, using it to smash the machine's control panel. The machine let out a loud whine, its lights flickering wildly as it began to malfunction.

Lady Arachne's eyes flashed with energy, and she let out a deafening roar. The ground began to shake, and the air was filled with an intense, pulsating energy.

Dr. Vraxxis stumbled back, her eyes fixed on Lady Arachne's transforming body. She knew that she had to get out of there, fast.

With a swift motion, Dr. Vraxxis turned and ran, dashing out of the room as fast as she could. She could hear Lady Arachne's roars echoing behind her, and the sound of the machine malfunctioning.

As she ran, Dr. Vraxxis knew that she had to find a way to stop Lady Arachne and the Architeuthis Zorvathii. She knew that she couldn't do it alone, and that she needed to find a way to gather a team of allies to help her.

With a determined look on her face, Dr. Vraxxis set out to gather a team of experts who could help her stop Lady Arachne and the Architeuthis Zorvathii. She knew that it wouldn't be easy, but she was determined to save the world from the alien entity's deadly grasp.

As she ran through the corridors, Dr. Vraxxis's mind was racing with thoughts of how to stop Lady Arachne and the Architeuthis Zorvathii. She knew that she had to act fast, before it was too late.

Suddenly, Dr. Vraxxis heard a voice behind her. "Dr. Vraxxis, wait!" it said.

Dr. Vraxxis turned to see a figure emerging from the shadows. It was Maya, her eyes flashing with determination.

"I'm not going to let you face this alone," Maya said. "We're in this together, now and forever."

Dr. Vraxxis smiled, a sense of relief washing over her. "Together, we can do this," she said.

And with that, Dr. Vraxxis and Maya set out on their mission to stop Lady Arachne and the Architeuthis Zorvathii. They knew that it wouldn't be easy, but they were determined to save the world from the alien entity's deadly grasp.

AS THEY JOURNEYED DEEPER into the heart of the lab, Dr. Vraxxis and Maya encountered more and more obstacles. They fought off hordes of heavily armed guards, dodged deadly traps, and navigated through treacherous corridors filled with toxic gases and hazardous materials.

Despite the dangers, they pressed on, driven by their determination to stop Lady Arachne and the Architeuthis Zorvathii. They knew that time was running out, and that they had to act fast if they were going to save the world.

As they turned a corner, they came face to face with Lady Arachne herself. She was standing in front of a massive, ancient-looking door, her eyes glowing with an otherworldly energy.

"Welcome, Dr. Vraxxis and Maya," Lady Arachne said, her voice dripping with malice. "I've been waiting for you. You're just in time to witness the birth of a new era."

Dr. Vraxxis's eyes narrowed. "We're not going to let you do it, Lady Arachne," she said. "We're going to stop you, no matter what it takes."

CROSSING THE COSMIC HORIZON

Lady Arachne laughed, a cold, mirthless sound. "You're no match for me," she said. "I have the power of the Architeuthis Zorvathii on my side. And with this machine, I'll be able to harness that power and use it to control the minds of world leaders."

Maya's eyes widened in horror. "You can't be serious," she said.

Lady Arachne's eyes flashed with energy. "I'm dead serious," she said. "And with this machine, I'll be able to make my vision a reality."

Dr. Vraxxis's face twisted with determination. "We're not going to let you do it," she said. "We're going to stop you, no matter what it takes."

With a fierce cry, Dr. Vraxxis and Maya charged forward, determined to stop Lady Arachne and the Architeuthis Zorvathii. But as they approached the machine, they were met with a shocking sight.

The machine was glowing with an intense, pulsating energy, and Lady Arachne was standing in front of it, her eyes flashing with power. The air around her was distorting and rippling, as if reality itself was bending to her will.

Dr. Vraxxis's eyes widened in horror. "What's happening?" she asked.

Lady Arachne's eyes flashed with energy. "The machine is activating," she said. "And with it, I'll be able to harness the power of the Architeuthis Zorvathii and use it to control the minds of world leaders."

Maya's eyes widened in horror. "We have to stop her," she said.

Dr. Vraxxis nodded, her face twisted with determination. "We will," she said. "No matter what it takes."

With a fierce cry, Dr. Vraxxis and Maya charged forward, determined to stop Lady Arachne and the Architeuthis Zorvathii. But as they approached the machine, they were met with a shocking sight.

The machine was glowing with an intense, pulsating energy, and Lady Arachne was standing in front of it, her eyes flashing with power.

The air around her was distorting and rippling, as if reality itself was bending to her will.

Dr. Vraxxis's eyes widened in horror. "What's happening?" she asked.

Lady Arachne's eyes flashed with energy. "The machine is activating," she said. "And with it, I'll be able to harness the power of the Architeuthis Zorvathii and use it to control the minds of world leaders."

Maya's eyes widened in horror. "We have to stop her," she said.

Dr. Vraxxis nodded, her face twisted with determination. "We will," she said. "No matter what it takes."

With a fierce cry, Dr. Vraxxis and Maya charged forward, determined to stop Lady Arachne and the Architeuthis Zorvathii. But as they approached the machine, they were met with a shocking sight.

The machine was glowing with an intense, pulsating energy, and Lady Arachne was standing in front of it, her eyes flashing with power. The air around her was distorting and rippling, as if reality itself was bending to her will.

Dr. Vraxxis's eyes widened in horror. "What's happening?" she asked.

Lady Arachne's eyes flashed with energy. "The machine is activating," she said. "And with it, I'll be able to harness the power of the Architeuthis Zorvathii and use it to control the minds of world leaders."

Maya's eyes widened in horror. "We have to stop her

MAYA'S EYES WIDENED in horror. "We have to stop her," she repeated, her voice shaking with urgency.

Dr. Vraxxis nodded, her face set in a determined expression. "We will," she said. "We have to."

CROSSING THE COSMIC HORIZON

With a fierce cry, Dr. Vraxxis and Maya charged forward, determined to stop Lady Arachne and the Architeuthis Zorvathii. They fought their way through the lab, taking down guards and dodging deadly traps.

As they approached the machine, they could feel the energy emanating from it growing stronger. The air around them seemed to distort and ripple, as if reality itself was bending to Lady Arachne's will.

Dr. Vraxxis and Maya exchanged a look, and then they charged forward, determined to stop Lady Arachne and the Architeuthis Zorvathii.

They fought their way through the lab, taking down guards and dodging deadly traps. They were determined to stop Lady Arachne and the Architeuthis Zorvathii, no matter what it took.

As they approached the machine, they could feel the energy emanating from it growing stronger. The air around them seemed to distort and ripple, as if reality itself was bending to Lady Arachne's will.

Dr. Vraxxis and Maya exchanged a look, and then they charged forward, determined to stop Lady Arachne and the Architeuthis Zorvathii.

They fought their way through the lab, taking down guards and dodging deadly traps. They were determined to stop Lady Arachne and the Architeuthis Zorvathii, no matter what it took.

As they approached the machine, Lady Arachne turned to face them. Her eyes were glowing with an otherworldly energy, and her skin was stretched taut over her skull.

"You fools," she spat. "You think you can stop me? I have the power of the Architeuthis Zorvathii on my side. I am unstoppable."

Dr. Vraxxis and Maya exchanged a look, and then they charged forward, determined to stop Lady Arachne and the Architeuthis Zorvathii.

They fought their way through the lab, taking down guards and dodging deadly traps. They were determined to stop Lady Arachne and the Architeuthis Zorvathii, no matter what it took.

As they approached the machine, Lady Arachne raised her hands, and a blast of energy shot out, striking Dr. Vraxxis and Maya with incredible force.

The two women stumbled back, their bodies battered and bruised. But they refused to give up. They knew that they had to stop Lady Arachne and the Architeuthis Zorvathii, no matter what it took.

With a fierce cry, Dr. Vraxxis and Maya charged forward, determined to stop Lady Arachne and the Architeuthis Zorvathii once and for all.

But as they approached the machine, they were met with a shocking sight. Lady Arachne was standing in front of the machine, her eyes glowing with an otherworldly energy.

And behind her, the machine was glowing with an intense, pulsating energy. The air around it seemed to distort and ripple, as if reality itself was bending to Lady Arachne's will.

Dr. Vraxxis and Maya exchanged a look, and then they charged forward, determined to stop Lady Arachne and the Architeuthis Zorvathii once and for all.

But as they approached the machine, they were met with a shocking sight. Lady Arachne was standing in front of the machine, her eyes glowing with an otherworldly energy.

And behind her, the machine was glowing with an intense, pulsating energy. The air around it seemed to distort and ripple, as if reality itself was bending to Lady Arachne's will.

Dr. Vraxxis and Maya exchanged a look, and then they charged forward, determined to stop Lady Arachne and the Architeuthis Zorvathii once and for all.

CROSSING THE COSMIC HORIZON

But as they approached the machine, Lady Arachne raised her hands, and a blast of energy shot out, striking Dr. Vraxxis and Maya with incredible force.

The two women stumbled back, their bodies battered and bruised. But they refused to give up. They knew that they had to stop Lady Arachne and the Architeuthis Zorvathii, no matter what it took.

With a fierce cry, Dr. Vraxxis and Maya charged forward, determined to stop Lady Arachne and the Architeuthis Zorvathii once and for all.

But as they approached the machine, they were met with a shocking sight. Lady Arachne was standing in front of the machine, her eyes glowing with an otherworldly energy.

And behind her, the machine was glowing with an

With a fierce cry, Dr. Vraxxis and Maya charged forward, determined to stop Lady Arachne and the Architeuthis Zorvathii once and for all.

Dr. Vraxxis launched herself at Lady Arachne, tackling her to the ground. The two women rolled around, punching and kicking each other. Maya joined the fight, using her agility and quick reflexes to dodge Lady Arachne's attacks.

As the three women fought, the machine behind them continued to glow with an intense, pulsating energy. The air around it seemed to distort and ripple, as if reality itself was bending to Lady Arachne's will.

But Dr. Vraxxis and Maya refused to give up. They fought with every ounce of strength they possessed, determined to stop Lady Arachne and the Architeuthis Zorvathii.

Finally, after what seemed like an eternity, Dr. Vraxxis managed to gain the upper hand. She pinned Lady Arachne to the ground, her hands wrapped tightly around her throat.

"It's over," Dr. Vraxxis said, her voice cold and deadly. "You're not going to use the Architeuthis Zorvathii to control the minds of world leaders. You're not going to use it to destroy the world."

Lady Arachne's eyes widened in horror as she realized that she was beaten. She tried to struggle, but Dr. Vraxxis's grip was too strong.

With a swift motion, Dr. Vraxxis snapped Lady Arachne's neck, ending her evil plans once and for all.

As Lady Arachne's body went limp, the machine behind her began to malfunction. The energy it was emitting began to build to a critical level, and the air around it began to distort and ripple even more violently.

Dr. Vraxxis and Maya exchanged a look, and then they turned and ran. They knew that they had to get out of the lab as quickly as possible, before the machine exploded and destroyed everything.

They ran as fast as they could, their hearts pounding in their chests. They could hear the machine behind them, its energy building to a critical level.

Finally, they reached the door of the lab and burst through it, slamming it shut behind them. They leaned against the door, panting heavily, as they waited for the machine to explode.

It didn't take long. A few seconds later, the machine exploded, destroying the lab and everything in it. Dr. Vraxxis and Maya stumbled back, their ears ringing from the blast.

As they looked at each other, they knew that they had saved the world from a terrible fate. They had stopped Lady Arachne and the Architeuthis Zorvathii, and they had destroyed the machine that would have allowed them to control the minds of world leaders.

Dr. Vraxxis smiled, a sense of pride and satisfaction washing over her. "We did it," she said. "We saved the world."

Maya nodded, a smile spreading across her face. "We make a pretty good team," she said.

Dr. Vraxxis chuckled. "We certainly do," she said.

As they walked away from the destroyed lab, Dr. Vraxxis and Maya knew that they would always stand together, ready to face whatever dangers lay ahead. They had saved the world, and they had saved each other.

And as they disappeared into the distance, the world was forever changed. The evil plans of Lady Arachne and the Architeuthis Zorvathii had been foiled, and the world was safe once again.

But as the dust settled, a strange, glowing artifact was left behind. It pulsed with an otherworldly energy, and it seemed to be calling out to something.

And as the artifact glowed brighter and brighter, a voice whispered in the darkness. "The Architeuthis Zorvathii will return," it said. "And next time, no one will be able to stop it."

The voice was low and menacing, and it sent a shiver down the spine of anyone who heard it. The artifact continued to glow brighter and brighter, and it seemed to be growing in power by the second.

Dr. Vraxxis and Maya were long gone, but they had left behind a team of scientists to study the artifact and try to understand its secrets. The scientists were led by a brilliant and fearless woman named Dr. Sophia Patel.

Dr. Patel was determined to unlock the secrets of the artifact, and she was willing to risk everything to do it. She assembled a team of experts in various fields, and together they began to study the artifact in depth.

As they worked, they began to realize the true extent of the artifact's power. It was not just a simple relic of an ancient civilization - it was a key to unlocking the secrets of the universe itself.

But as they delved deeper into their research, they began to realize that they were not alone. There were others out there who were also searching for the artifact, and they would stop at nothing to get it.

Dr. Patel and her team knew that they had to be careful. They were playing with forces beyond their control, and they knew that they could easily unleash a disaster of epic proportions.

But they were driven by their curiosity and their desire for knowledge. They were determined to unlock the secrets of the artifact, no matter what the cost.

And so they continued their research, pouring all of their energy into unlocking the secrets of the artifact. They worked tirelessly, day and night, driven by their passion for discovery.

But as they worked, they began to realize that they were in over their heads. The artifact was more powerful than they had ever imagined, and they were beginning to lose control of it.

Dr. Patel knew that they had to act fast. She called an emergency meeting with her team, and they gathered around the artifact, their faces filled with concern.

"We have to shut it down," Dr. Patel said, her voice firm and decisive. "We can't let it continue to grow in power. We don't know what it's capable of, and we can't take the risk."

But as they tried to shut down the artifact, they realized that it was too late. The artifact had already reached a critical point, and it was now beyond their control.

The room began to shake and tremble, and the air was filled with an intense, pulsating energy. The artifact was glowing brighter and brighter, and it seemed to be growing in power by the second.

Dr. Patel and her team knew that they had to get out of there, fast. They turned and ran, but it was too late. The artifact exploded in a blast of energy, destroying the lab and everything in it.

As the dust settled, Dr. Patel and her team stumbled out of the wreckage, their faces filled with shock and horror. They knew that they had unleashed a disaster of epic proportions, and they didn't know how to stop it.

The artifact's energy was still pulsating through the air, and it seemed to be growing in power by the second. Dr. Patel and her team knew that they had to act fast, or risk losing everything.

CROSSING THE COSMIC HORIZON

But as they looked around, they realized that they were not alone. There were others out there, watching them, waiting for them to make their next move.

And Dr. Patel knew that they were in grave danger. The artifact's energy was still pulsating through the air, and it seemed to be calling out to something.

Something that was coming for them, something that would stop at nothing to claim the artifact's power for itself.

Dr. Patel's eyes narrowed, her mind racing with thoughts of what was to come. She knew that they had to be prepared, that they had to be ready to face whatever dangers lay ahead.

And so she gathered her team around her, her eyes locked on theirs. "We have to be ready," she said, her voice firm and decisive. "We have to be prepared to face whatever is coming for us."

And with that, they set to work, gathering their strength and preparing for the battle that was to come. They knew that it would be a fight to the death, but they were ready.

For they knew that they were the only ones who could stop the artifact's power from falling into the wrong hands. And they were determined to do whatever it took to protect the world from the dangers that lay ahead.

As they prepared for the battle ahead, Dr. Patel and her team knew that they had to be strategic. They gathered all the information they could about the artifact and its power, and they studied the ancient texts that held the secrets of the Architeuthis Zorvathii.

They also knew that they had to be prepared for the unexpected. They gathered all the equipment they could, from high-tech gadgets to ancient artifacts, and they trained themselves in every form of combat they could think of.

As they worked, they could feel the power of the artifact growing stronger. It was as if it was calling out to them, tempting them to use its power for their own gain.

But Dr. Patel and her team were not tempted. They knew that the artifact's power was too great for any one person to wield, and they were determined to stop it from falling into the wrong hands.

As they finished their preparations, Dr. Patel stood up and looked at her team. "We're ready," she said. "Let's do this."

And with that, they set out to face whatever dangers lay ahead. They knew that it would be a difficult battle, but they were determined to win.

As they journeyed deeper into the heart of the artifact's power, they encountered all manner of dangers. They fought off hordes of twisted creatures, and they navigated treacherous landscapes filled with deadly traps and puzzles.

But they persevered, using all of their skills and knowledge to overcome every obstacle. And finally, after what seemed like an eternity, they reached the heart of the artifact's power.

It was a great crystal temple, filled with ancient artifacts and mysterious energy. And at the center of it all was the artifact itself, glowing with an intense, pulsating energy.

Dr. Patel and her team approached the artifact cautiously, their hearts pounding with excitement and fear. They knew that this was it – this was the moment they had been preparing for.

And as they reached out to touch the artifact, they felt a sudden surge of energy. The artifact began to glow even brighter, and the air around them seemed to distort and ripple.

Dr. Patel and her team stumbled back, their eyes wide with wonder. They knew that they had unleashed a power that was beyond their control.

And as they watched, the artifact began to transform. It grew larger and more powerful, its energy pulsating through the air like a living thing.

CROSSING THE COSMIC HORIZON

Dr. Patel and her team knew that they had to act fast. They gathered all of their equipment and prepared to face whatever dangers lay ahead.

And as they stood there, ready to face the unknown, the artifact spoke to them in a voice that was both ancient and eternal.

"You have unleashed my power," it said. "Now you must face the consequences."

And with that, the artifact unleashed a blast of energy that sent Dr. Patel and her team flying across the room. They landed hard on the stone floor, dazed and disoriented.

As they struggled to get to their feet, they saw the artifact begin to transform even further. It grew larger and more powerful, its energy pulsating through the air like a living thing.

Dr. Patel and her team knew that they had to act fast. They gathered all of their equipment and prepared to face whatever dangers lay ahead.

And as they stood there, ready to face the unknown, the artifact spoke to them again.

"You have unleashed my power," it said. "Now you must face the consequences."

And with that, the artifact unleashed a blast of energy that sent Dr. Patel and her team flying across the room. They landed hard on the stone floor, dazed and disoriented.

As they struggled to get to their feet, they saw the artifact begin to transform even further. It grew larger and more powerful, its energy pulsating through the air like a living thing.

Dr. Patel and her team knew that they had to act fast. They gathered all of their equipment and prepared to face whatever dangers lay ahead.

And as they stood there, ready to face the unknown, the artifact spoke to them again.

"You have unleashed my power," it said. "Now you must face the consequences."

And with that, the artifact unleashed a blast of energy that sent Dr. Patel and her team flying across the room. They landed hard on the stone floor, dazed and disoriented.

As they struggled to get to their feet, they saw the artifact begin to transform even further. It grew larger and more powerful, its energy pulsating through the air like a living thing.

Dr. Patel and her team knew that they had to act fast. They gathered all of their equipment and prepared to face whatever dangers lay ahead.

And as they stood there, ready to face the unknown, the artifact spoke to them again.

"You have unleashed my power," it said. "Now you must face the consequences."

And with that, the artifact unleashed a blast of energy that sent Dr. Patel and her team flying across the room. They landed hard on the stone floor, dazed and dis

As they struggled to get to their feet, they saw the artifact begin to transform even further. It grew larger and more powerful, its energy pulsating through the air like a living thing.

Dr. Patel and her team knew that they had to act fast. They gathered all of their equipment and prepared to face whatever dangers lay ahead.

"We have to destroy it," Dr. Patel said, her voice firm and decisive. "We can't let it continue to grow in power."

But as they approached the artifact, they realized that it was not going to be easy. The artifact was surrounded by a powerful energy field, and it seemed to be absorbing all of the energy around it.

"We need to find a way to disable the energy field," one of the team members said. "If we can do that, we might be able to destroy the artifact."

CROSSING THE COSMIC HORIZON

Dr. Patel nodded, her mind racing with possibilities. "Let's get to work," she said. "We don't have much time."

The team quickly got to work, using all of their knowledge and skills to try and disable the energy field. They worked tirelessly, pouring all of their energy into the task.

And finally, after what seemed like an eternity, they succeeded. The energy field surrounding the artifact began to falter, and the team knew that they had their chance.

With a fierce cry, they launched themselves at the artifact, determined to destroy it once and for all. The artifact let out a deafening roar as they attacked, but the team refused to back down.

They fought with every ounce of strength they possessed, using all of their knowledge and skills to try and destroy the artifact. And finally, after what seemed like an eternity, they succeeded.

The artifact let out a final, defeated roar, and then it was silent. The team stood panting, their chests heaving with exhaustion.

They had done it. They had destroyed the artifact, and they had saved the world from its evil power.

But as they stood there, basking in the glow of their victory, they couldn't shake the feeling that they had only just begun to scratch the surface of a much larger, much more sinister plot.

And as they turned to leave, they saw a figure watching them from the shadows. A figure with piercing eyes, and a smile that sent shivers down their spines.

"You may have won this battle," the figure said, its voice dripping with malice. "But the war is far from over."

And with that, the figure vanished into the shadows, leaving Dr. Patel and her team to wonder what other dangers lay ahead.

As the figure vanished into the shadows, Dr. Patel and her team were left with a sense of unease. They knew that they had just scratched the surface of a much larger, more complex plot.

"Who was that?" one of the team members asked, her voice barely above a whisper.

Dr. Patel shook her head. "I don't know," she said. "But I think we're about to find out."

As they turned to leave, they were confronted by a group of heavily armed guards. The guards were dressed in black tactical gear, and their faces were obscured by masks.

"Dr. Patel," one of the guards said, his voice firm and authoritative. "You and your team are coming with us."

Dr. Patel's eyes narrowed. "Who are you?" she demanded. "What do you want?"

The guard smiled, his eyes glinting with amusement. "We're here to take you to someone who wants to meet you," he said. "Someone who has been waiting for you for a very long time."

Dr. Patel's eyes widened as she realized who the guard might be talking about. "No," she whispered. "It can't be."

The guard smiled again, his eyes glinting with amusement. "Oh, but it can," he said. "And it is."

With that, the guard reached out and grabbed Dr. Patel, pulling her away from her team. Dr. Patel struggled and kicked, but the guard was too strong. He dragged her away, leaving her team to wonder what was happening.

As they were dragged deeper into the complex, Dr. Patel saw that they were surrounded by more and more guards. She realized that they were in grave danger, and that they had to escape.

But as they turned a corner, Dr. Patel saw a figure waiting for them. A figure with piercing eyes, and a smile that sent shivers down her spine.

"Welcome, Dr. Patel," the figure said, its voice dripping with malice. "I've been waiting for you."

Dr. Patel's eyes widened as she realized who the figure was. "You're...you're the one who's been behind all of this," she stammered.

CROSSING THE COSMIC HORIZON

The figure smiled, its eyes glinting with amusement. "I am," it said. "And now, you're going to help me achieve my ultimate goal."

Dr. Patel's eyes narrowed. "I'll never help you," she spat.

The figure smiled again, its eyes glinting with amusement. "Oh, but you will," it said. "You'll do exactly what I say, or else."

Dr. Patel's eyes widened as she realized what the figure was implying. "You wouldn't dare," she whispered.

The figure smiled again, its eyes glinting with amusement. "Oh, but I would," it said. "And I will."

And with that, the figure reached out and grabbed Dr. Patel, pulling her away from her team. Dr. Patel struggled and kicked, but the figure was too strong. It dragged her away, leaving her team to wonder what was happening.

As they were dragged deeper into the complex, Dr. Patel saw that they were surrounded by more and more guards. She realized that they were in grave danger, and that they had to escape.

But as they turned a corner, Dr. Patel saw a figure waiting for them. A figure with piercing eyes, and a smile that sent shivers down her spine.

"Welcome, Dr. Patel," the figure said, its voice dripping with malice. "I've been waiting for you."

Dr. Patel's eyes widened as she realized who the figure was. "You're...you're the one who's been behind all of this," she stammered.

The figure smiled, its eyes glinting with amusement. "I am," it said. "And now, you're going to help me achieve my ultimate goal."

Dr. Patel's eyes narrowed. "I'll never help you," she spat.

The figure smiled again, its eyes glinting with amusement. "Oh, but you will," it said. "You'll do exactly what I say, or else."

Dr. Patel's eyes widened as she realized what the figure was implying. "You wouldn't dare," she whispered.

The figure smiled again, its eyes glinting with amusement. "Oh, but I would," it said. "And I will."

And with that, the figure reached out and grabbed Dr. Patel, pulling her away from her team. Dr. Patel struggled and kicked, but the figure was too strong. It dragged her away, leaving her team to wonder what was happening.

As they were dragged deeper into the complex, Dr. Patel saw that they were surrounded by more and more guards. She realized that they were in grave danger, and that they had to escape.

But as they turned a corner, Dr. Patel saw a figure waiting for them. A figure with piercing eyes, and a

A figure with piercing eyes, and a smile that sent shivers down her spine.

"Welcome, Dr. Patel," the figure said, its voice dripping with malice. "I've been waiting for you."

Dr. Patel's eyes widened as she realized who the figure was. "You're...you're the one who's been behind all of this," she stammered.

The figure smiled, its eyes glinting with amusement. "I am," it said. "And now, you're going to help me achieve my ultimate goal."

Dr. Patel's eyes narrowed. "I'll never help you," she spat.

The figure smiled again, its eyes glinting with amusement. "Oh, but you will," it said. "You'll do exactly what I say, or else."

Dr. Patel's eyes widened as she realized what the figure was implying. "You wouldn't dare," she whispered.

The figure smiled again, its eyes glinting with amusement. "Oh, but I would," it said. "And I will."

And with that, the figure reached out and grabbed Dr. Patel, pulling her away from her team. Dr. Patel struggled and kicked, but the figure was too strong. It dragged her away, leaving her team to wonder what was happening.

As they were dragged deeper into the complex, Dr. Patel saw that they were surrounded by more and more guards. She realized that they were in grave danger, and that they had to escape.

But as they turned a corner, Dr. Patel saw a figure waiting for them. A figure with piercing eyes, and a smile that sent shivers down her spine.

"Welcome, Dr. Patel," the figure said, its voice dripping with malice. "I've been waiting for you."

Dr. Patel's eyes widened as she realized who the figure was. "You're...you're the one who's been behind all of this," she stammered.

The figure smiled, its eyes glinting with amusement. "I am," it said. "And now, you're going to help me achieve my ultimate goal."

Dr. Patel's eyes narrowed. "I'll never help you," she spat.

The figure smiled again, its eyes glinting with amusement. "Oh, but you will," it said. "You'll do exactly what I say, or else."

Dr. Patel's eyes widened as she realized what the figure was implying. "You wouldn't dare," she whispered.

The figure smiled again, its eyes glinting with amusement. "Oh, but I would," it said. "And I will."

And with that, the figure reached out and grabbed Dr. Patel, pulling her away from her team. Dr. Patel struggled and kicked, but the figure was too strong. It dragged her away, leaving her team to wonder what was happening.

As they were dragged deeper into the complex, Dr. Patel saw that they were surrounded by more and more guards. She realized that they were in grave danger, and that they had to escape.

But as they turned a corner, Dr. Patel saw a figure waiting for them. A figure with piercing eyes, and a smile that sent shivers down her spine.

"Welcome, Dr. Patel," the figure said, its voice dripping with malice. "I've been waiting for you."

Dr. Patel's eyes widened as she realized who the figure was. "You're...you're the one who's been behind all of this," she stammered.

The figure smiled, its eyes glinting with amusement. "I am," it said. "And now, you're going to help me achieve my ultimate goal."

Dr. Patel's eyes narrowed. "I'll never help you," she spat.

The figure smiled again, its eyes glinting with amusement. "Oh, but you will," it said. "You'll do exactly what I say, or else."

Dr. Patel's eyes widened as she realized what the figure was implying. "You wouldn't dare," she whispered.

The figure smiled again, its eyes glinting with amusement. "Oh, but I would," it said. "And I will."

And with that, the figure reached out and grabbed Dr. Patel, pulling her away from her team. Dr. Patel struggled and kicked, but the figure was too strong. It dragged her away, leaving her team to wonder what was happening.

As they were dragged deeper into the complex, Dr. Patel saw that they were surrounded by more and more guards. She realized that they were in grave danger, and that they had to escape.

But as they turned a corner, Dr. Patel saw a figure waiting for them. A figure with piercing eyes, and a smile that sent shivers down her spine.

"Welcome, Dr. Patel," the figure said, its voice dripping with malice. "I've been waiting for you."

Dr. Patel's eyes widened as she realized who the figure was. "You're..."

"You're...the one they call 'The Archon,'" Dr. Patel stammered.

The figure nodded, its smile growing wider. "I am," it said. "And I have been waiting for you, Dr. Patel. You have something that belongs to me, something that will help me achieve my ultimate goal."

Dr. Patel's eyes narrowed. "I don't know what you're talking about," she said.

The Archon laughed, its eyes glinting with amusement. "Don't play dumb, Dr. Patel," it said. "I know all about the artifact. I know that you and your team have been studying it, trying to unlock its secrets."

Dr. Patel's eyes widened as she realized that The Archon was telling the truth. "How did you know?" she asked.

CROSSING THE COSMIC HORIZON

The Archon smiled again. "I have my ways," it said. "And now, I want the artifact. I want it, and I will stop at nothing to get it."

Dr. Patel's eyes narrowed. "You'll never get it," she said. "I'll never let you have it."

The Archon laughed again, its eyes glinting with amusement. "We'll see about that," it said. "Guards, take Dr. Patel to the holding cell. We'll see how long she lasts without her precious artifact."

The guards moved forward, grabbing Dr. Patel and dragging her away. She struggled and kicked, but they were too strong. They threw her into a cell, slamming the door shut behind her.

Dr. Patel sat on the floor, her eyes fixed on the door. She knew that she had to escape, had to get back to her team and stop The Archon's evil plans.

But as she looked around the cell, she realized that it wasn't going to be easy. The walls were thick and solid, the door was made of steel, and the guards were patrolling the corridors outside.

Dr. Patel's eyes narrowed. She knew that she had to think, had to come up with a plan. And she knew that she had to act fast, before The Archon could carry out its evil plans.

As she sat in the darkness, Dr. Patel's mind began to spin. She thought about the artifact, about its power and its secrets. She thought about The Archon, about its plans and its motivations.

And then, suddenly, she had an idea. A plan began to form in her mind, a plan that would allow her to escape, to stop The Archon, and to save the world.

Dr. Patel's eyes gleamed with determination. She knew that it wouldn't be easy, but she was ready. She was ready to face whatever challenges lay ahead, to fight for what was right, and to save the world from The Archon's evil plans.

DR. PATEL'S EYES GLEAMED with determination as she began to put her plan into action. She knew that she had to be careful, that one misstep could mean capture or worse.

She started by examining her cell, looking for any weaknesses or vulnerabilities. She checked the walls, the floor, and the ceiling, searching for any possible means of escape.

As she searched, she noticed a small ventilation shaft in the wall. It was narrow, but it looked like it might be just large enough for her to fit through.

Dr. Patel's heart began to pound with excitement. She knew that this could be her only chance to escape.

She carefully made her way over to the ventilation shaft, trying not to make any noise. She reached up and grabbed the edge of the shaft, pulling herself up and into the narrow opening.

As she crawled through the shaft, Dr. Patel could feel her heart pounding in her chest. She was scared, but she was also determined. She knew that she had to keep moving, had to keep pushing forward.

Finally, after what seemed like an eternity, Dr. Patel saw a glimmer of light ahead. She crawled towards it, her heart pounding with excitement.

As she emerged from the ventilation shaft, Dr. Patel found herself in a long, dark corridor. She could hear the sound of guards patrolling the area, but she knew that she had to keep moving.

She started to run, her feet pounding the floor as she sprinted down the corridor. She could hear the guards behind her, but she didn't look back. She kept her eyes fixed on the door ahead, her heart pounding with excitement.

Finally, she reached the door and burst through it, finding herself in a crowded street. She could see people milling around, going about their daily business.

CROSSING THE COSMIC HORIZON

Dr. Patel's eyes scanned the crowd, searching for any sign of her team. She knew that they had to be somewhere, had to be waiting for her.

And then, suddenly, she saw them. Maya and the others were standing across the street, their eyes fixed on her.

Dr. Patel's heart leapt with joy. She knew that she had made it, had escaped from The Archon's clutches.

She started to run towards her team, her feet pounding the pavement. She could hear the guards behind her, but she didn't look back. She kept her eyes fixed on her team, her heart pounding with excitement.

As she reached her team, Dr. Patel was swept up in a flurry of hugs and congratulations. Maya and the others were overjoyed to see her, to know that she was safe.

But Dr. Patel knew that they couldn't celebrate yet. They still had to stop The Archon, had to prevent it from carrying out its evil plans.

"We have to get out of here," Dr. Patel said, her voice urgent. "We have to stop The Archon before it's too late."

Maya and the others nodded, their faces set with determination. They knew that they had a long and difficult road ahead of them, but they were ready.

Together, they set off into the unknown, determined to stop The Archon and save the world.

As they navigated through the crowded streets, Dr. Patel and her team knew they had to move quickly. They had to stop The Archon before it could carry out its plans.

"We need to get to the artifact," Dr. Patel said, her voice urgent. "We have to destroy it before The Archon can use it."

Maya nodded, her eyes scanning the crowd. "I know where it is," she said. "Follow me."

They weaved through the crowded streets, Maya leading the way. They finally reached a small, nondescript building, and Maya pushed open the door.

Inside, they found themselves in a dimly lit room, the artifact sitting on a pedestal in the center of the room. Dr. Patel's eyes widened as she saw it, her heart racing with excitement.

"We have to destroy it," she said, her voice firm. "We can't let The Archon use it."

Maya nodded, her eyes fixed on the artifact. "I'll take care of it," she said.

As Maya reached out to touch the artifact, a loud noise echoed through the room. The Archon had found them.

"Too late," a voice said, echoing off the walls. "You'll never stop me now."

Dr. Patel turned to see The Archon standing in the doorway, its eyes blazing with fury.

"We'll never give up," Dr. Patel said, her voice firm. "We'll stop you, no matter what it takes."

The Archon laughed, its eyes glinting with amusement. "We'll see about that," it said.

And with that, The Archon raised its hand, and a blast of energy shot towards Dr. Patel and her team. They dodged and weaved, avoiding the energy blasts, but they knew they couldn't keep this up for much longer.

They had to come up with a plan, and fast. They had to stop The Archon, and destroy the artifact once and for all.

But as they looked at each other, they knew they were in trouble. They were outnumbered, outgunned, and out of options.

Or so it seemed.

Dr. Patel's eyes narrowed, a plan forming in her mind. "I think I have an idea," she said, her voice low and urgent.

CROSSING THE COSMIC HORIZON

Maya and the others looked at her, their eyes filled with hope. "What is it?" Maya asked.

Dr. Patel smiled, a fierce determination burning in her eyes. "We're going to use the artifact against The Archon," she said.

The others stared at her in shock, but Dr. Patel just smiled. "Trust me," she said. "It's the only way we're going to stop The Archon and save the world."

DR. PATEL TOOK A DEEP breath and began to explain the artifact's true nature.

"The artifact is an ancient relic known as the 'Erebus Engine,'" she said. "It's a device that has the power to manipulate reality itself. It was created by an ancient civilization that possessed technology and knowledge far beyond our own."

Maya's eyes widened in amazement. "That's incredible," she said. "But what does it do exactly?"

Dr. Patel's expression turned serious. "The Erebus Engine has the power to warp space-time, creating portals to other dimensions and allowing for faster-than-light travel. But it also has a darker side. It can be used to manipulate the fabric of reality, creating illusions and distortions that can be used to control and deceive others."

The others looked at each other in alarm. "That's terrifying," one of them said. "If The Archon gets its hands on that kind of power, it could be catastrophic."

Dr. Patel nodded. "That's why we have to stop it," she said. "We can't let The Archon use the Erebus Engine to manipulate reality and bend the world to its will."

Maya's eyes narrowed. "But how do we stop it?" she asked. "We can't just destroy the artifact. We need to find a way to neutralize its power."

Dr. Patel smiled. "I think I have an idea," she said. "We can use the artifact's own power against it. We can create a resonance frequency that will disrupt the Erebus Engine's energy matrix, rendering it useless."

The others looked at each other in surprise. "That's genius," one of them said. "But can we do it in time?"

Dr. Patel's expression turned determined. "We have to try," she said. "We owe it to ourselves, to each other, and to the world to stop The Archon and destroy the Erebus Engine once and for all."

With a newfound sense of determination, Dr. Patel and her team set to work on creating the resonance frequency that would disrupt the Erebus Engine's energy matrix.

They worked tirelessly, pouring all of their knowledge and expertise into the task. They gathered equipment and materials, set up complex calculations and simulations, and worked through the night to fine-tune their plan.

As the hours ticked by, the tension in the room grew. They knew that they were running out of time, that The Archon could return at any moment to claim the Erebus Engine.

But Dr. Patel and her team refused to give up. They worked with a fierce dedication, driven by their determination to stop The Archon and save the world.

Finally, after what seemed like an eternity, they were ready. They stood before the Erebus Engine, their equipment at the ready.

"Here we go," Dr. Patel said, her voice steady and calm. "Let's do this."

With a nod, Maya activated the device, sending a blast of energy towards the Erebus Engine. The air around them seemed to vibrate with energy as the resonance frequency took hold.

The Erebus Engine began to glow with an intense, pulsating light. The energy matrix surrounding it began to distort and ripple, like the surface of a pond struck by a stone.

"It's working," Dr. Patel exclaimed, her eyes shining with excitement. "We're disrupting the energy matrix!"

CROSSING THE COSMIC HORIZON

But just as it seemed like they were on the verge of success, The Archon appeared, its eyes blazing with fury.

"You fools," it spat, its voice dripping with venom. "You think you can stop me? I am The Archon, and I will not be defeated!"

With a wave of its hand, The Archon sent a blast of energy towards Dr. Patel and her team. They stumbled back, shielding their eyes from the intense light.

But Dr. Patel refused to give up. With a fierce determination, she rallied her team and launched a counterattack.

The battle was fierce and intense, with energy blasts flying back and forth through the air. Dr. Patel and her team fought with all their might, determined to stop The Archon and destroy the Erebus Engine.

But as the fight raged on, it seemed like the odds were stacked against them. The Archon was too powerful, too relentless. It seemed like nothing could stop it.

And then, just when all hope seemed lost, Dr. Patel remembered something. She remembered the words of an ancient text, a text that spoke of the Erebus Engine's greatest weakness.

With a newfound sense of hope, Dr. Patel turned to her team and shouted, "We can do this! We can stop The Archon and destroy the Erebus Engine!"

But as she turned to face The Archon, she saw something that made her blood run cold. The Archon was not alone. It was surrounded by an army of twisted, corrupted creatures, creatures that seemed to be made of the very fabric of reality itself.

Dr. Patel's eyes widened in horror as she realized the true extent of The Archon's power. She knew that they were in grave danger, that they might not survive the battle ahead.

But she refused to give up. With a fierce determination, she rallied her team and prepared to face the army of corrupted creatures.

The battle was about to begin. The fate of the world hung in the balance. And Dr. Patel and her team were ready to fight.

The battle was intense and chaotic, with energy blasts flying back and forth through the air. Dr. Patel and her team fought with all their might, using every trick and tactic they knew to try and defeat the army of corrupted creatures.

But despite their best efforts, they were vastly outnumbered. The creatures seemed to be endless, pouring in from all sides like a tidal wave of twisted flesh and energy.

Dr. Patel stumbled back, her eyes scanning the battlefield in desperation. They were losing, and they were losing badly.

And then, just when all hope seemed lost, she saw something that gave her a glimmer of hope. Maya, her team member, was standing tall, her eyes blazing with determination.

Maya was holding a small device, a device that Dr. Patel recognized as a resonance generator. It was a device that could amplify the resonance frequency of the Erebus Engine, disrupting its energy matrix and rendering it useless.

Dr. Patel's eyes locked onto Maya's, and she nodded. Maya understood, and with a fierce cry, she activated the device.

The resonance generator emitted a blast of energy that resonated with the Erebus Engine's frequency. The engine's energy matrix began to distort and ripple, and the corrupted creatures began to stumble and fall.

Dr. Patel and her team took advantage of the distraction, launching a fierce counterattack against the creatures. The battle was intense and chaotic, but with the resonance generator's help, they were finally able to gain the upper hand.

As the last of the creatures fell, Dr. Patel turned to Maya with a grateful smile. "Thank you," she said. "We couldn't have done it without you."

Maya smiled back, her eyes shining with pride. "We make a good team," she said.

CROSSING THE COSMIC HORIZON

Dr. Patel nodded, her eyes scanning the battlefield. The Erebus Engine was still active, but it was no longer a threat. The resonance generator had disrupted its energy matrix, rendering it useless.

But as she turned to leave, Dr. Patel saw something that made her blood run cold. The Archon was standing behind her, its eyes blazing with fury.

"You may have won this battle," it spat, its voice dripping with venom. "But the war is far from over. I will return, and next time, you will not be so lucky."

Dr. Patel stood tall, her eyes locked onto The Archon's. "We'll be ready," she said, her voice firm and resolute.

The Archon sneered, its eyes flashing with anger. And then, in an instant, it vanished.

Dr. Patel let out a breath, her eyes scanning the battlefield. They had won, but at what cost? The world was still in danger, and The Archon was still out there, waiting for its next opportunity to strike.

But Dr. Patel was not afraid. She knew that she and her team had saved the world, at least for now. And she knew that they would be ready, whenever The Archon returned.

The battle was over, but the war was far from won. Dr. Patel and her team had saved the world, but they knew that they would have to fight again, soon.

As the dust settled, Dr. Patel and her team began to survey the damage. The laboratory was in shambles, equipment destroyed and debris scattered everywhere.

But despite the destruction, Dr. Patel felt a sense of pride and accomplishment. They had saved the world from The Archon's evil plans, at least for now.

As they began to clean up the mess, Maya approached Dr. Patel with a concerned look on her face.

"Dr. Patel, we need to talk," Maya said, her voice low and serious.

Dr. Patel looked at her, curious. "What is it, Maya?" she asked.

Maya hesitated, as if unsure of how to proceed. "It's about the Erebus Engine," she said finally. "I think we may have made a mistake by destroying it."

Dr. Patel's eyes widened in surprise. "What do you mean?" she asked.

Maya took a deep breath before speaking. "I've been going over the data we collected from the engine, and I think I may have found something. The engine wasn't just a simple device - it was a key part of a much larger system."

Dr. Patel's eyes narrowed. "What kind of system?" she asked.

Maya hesitated again, as if unsure of how to proceed. "I think the Erebus Engine was part of a system that could manipulate reality itself," she said finally. "And I think we may have just made things worse by destroying it."

Dr. Patel's eyes widened in shock. "What do you mean?" she asked.

Maya's voice was barely above a whisper. "I think we may have unleashed a power that we can't control. A power that could destroy the very fabric of reality itself."

Dr. Patel's face went pale as she realized the implications of Maya's words. They had thought they were saving the world, but they may have just made things worse.

As the reality of their situation sunk in, Dr. Patel and her team stood in stunned silence, unsure of what to do next.

As the reality of their situation sunk in, Dr. Patel and her team stood in stunned silence, unsure of what to do next. They had thought they were saving the world, but now they were faced with the possibility that they had made things worse.

Dr. Patel was the first to break the silence. "We need to figure out what's happening," she said, her voice firm and resolute. "We need to understand the implications of what we've done."

CROSSING THE COSMIC HORIZON

Maya nodded, her eyes already scanning the data on her tablet. "I'm on it," she said. "But we need to be careful. If what I think is happening is true, we could be facing a catastrophe of unimaginable proportions."

Dr. Patel's eyes narrowed. "What kind of catastrophe?" she asked.

Maya hesitated, as if unsure of how to answer. "I think we may have unleashed a reality distortion wave," she said finally. "A wave that could alter the very fabric of reality itself."

Dr. Patel's face went pale. "That's impossible," she whispered. "We can't have done that."

Maya's expression was grim. "I'm afraid we did," she said. "And now we have to figure out how to stop it."

As the team began to brainstorm ways to stop the reality distortion wave, Dr. Patel couldn't shake the feeling that they were in over their heads. They had thought they were saving the world, but now they were faced with the possibility that they had made things worse.

And as they worked to find a solution, Dr. Patel couldn't help but wonder if they would be able to fix the damage they had done. Or if it was already too late.

The team worked tirelessly, pouring over data and running simulations. But as the hours ticked by, Dr. Patel couldn't shake the feeling that they were running out of time.

And then, just as they were starting to make progress, the lab was rocked by a massive explosion. The team stumbled, caught off guard by the sudden blast.

As they struggled to regain their footing, Dr. Patel saw a figure emerging from the smoke. It was The Archon, its eyes blazing with fury.

"You fools," it spat, its voice dripping with venom. "You think you can stop me? I am The Archon, and I will not be defeated!"

Dr. Patel stood tall, her eyes locked onto The Archon's. "We'll never give up," she said, her voice firm and resolute.

The Archon sneered, its eyes flashing with anger. "We'll see about that," it said.

And with that, the battle began. Dr. Patel and her team fought with all their might, determined to stop The Archon and save the world.

But as the fight raged on, Dr. Patel couldn't shake the feeling that they were in grave danger. The Archon was powerful, and it would stop at nothing to achieve its goals.

And as the team fought to survive, Dr. Patel couldn't help but wonder if they would be able to emerge victorious. Or if The Archon would ultimately prove to be too powerful to defeat.

As the battle raged on, Dr. Patel and her team fought with all their might. They used every trick and tactic they knew, but The Archon seemed to be absorbing their attacks, growing stronger with each passing moment.

Dr. Patel's eyes locked onto The Archon's, and she knew that she had to think of something, and fast. She remembered the data they had collected on the Erebus Engine, and a plan began to form in her mind.

"Maya, can you hack into the lab's mainframe?" Dr. Patel asked, her voice urgent.

Maya nodded, her fingers flying across her tablet. "I'm in," she said. "What do you need me to do?"

Dr. Patel's eyes never left The Archon's. "I need you to activate the lab's self-destruct sequence," she said. "We have to destroy The Archon, no matter what it takes."

Maya's eyes widened, but she nodded. "I'm on it," she said.

As Maya worked to activate the self-destruct sequence, Dr. Patel and the rest of the team launched a final, desperate attack on The Archon. They fought with all their might, but The Archon seemed to be absorbing their attacks, growing stronger with each passing moment.

And then, just as all hope seemed lost, the lab's self-destruct sequence activated. A countdown timer appeared on the screens around the room, and Dr. Patel knew that they had to get out, fast.

CROSSING THE COSMIC HORIZON

"Everyone, we have to go, now!" Dr. Patel shouted, grabbing Maya's arm and pulling her towards the door.

The team followed close behind, fighting to stay ahead of The Archon as they made their way through the lab. They could hear the countdown timer ticking away, and they knew that they had to move fast if they wanted to survive.

As they burst through the door and into the hallway, Dr. Patel could feel the lab's self-destruct sequence counting down. She knew that they had to get as far away from the lab as possible, and fast.

"Keep moving!" Dr. Patel shouted, pushing the team forward. "We have to get out of here, now!"

The team sprinted down the hallway, their footsteps echoing off the walls. They could hear the countdown timer ticking away, and they knew that they were running out of time.

And then, just as they reached the exit, the lab's self-destruct sequence reached zero. The lab erupted in a massive explosion, sending debris flying everywhere.

Dr. Patel and her team stumbled out into the bright sunlight, gasping for air. They looked back at the lab, watching as it was consumed by flames.

"It's over," Dr. Patel said, her voice barely above a whisper. "We did it. We stopped The Archon."

But as they turned to walk away, Dr. Patel couldn't shake the feeling that they had only just begun to scratch the surface of a much larger, more complex problem.

And as they walked off into the distance, Dr. Patel couldn't help but wonder what other secrets lay hidden, waiting to be uncovered.

As they walked away from the burning lab, Dr. Patel couldn't shake the feeling that they had only just begun to scratch the surface of a much larger, more complex problem.

"What's next?" Maya asked, breaking the silence.

Dr. Patel hesitated, unsure of how to answer. "I'm not sure," she said finally. "We need to regroup and figure out our next move."

Maya nodded, her eyes scanning the surrounding area. "We need to get out of here," she said. "The authorities will be arriving soon, and we don't want to be here when they do."

Dr. Patel nodded, her mind racing with thoughts of their next move. They had stopped The Archon, but they knew that there were still many unanswered questions.

As they made their way through the streets, Dr. Patel's phone suddenly buzzed with an incoming call. She hesitated for a moment before answering.

"Hello?" she said, her voice cautious.

"Dr. Patel, it's Agent Thompson," a voice said on the other end of the line. "I've been trying to reach you. We've received reports of a massive explosion at the lab. What's going on?"

Dr. Patel hesitated, unsure of how much to reveal. "It's a long story," she said finally. "But we've stopped The Archon. At least, we think we have."

There was a pause on the other end of the line. "I see," Agent Thompson said finally. "Well, we'll need to debrief you and your team as soon as possible. Can you meet me at the safe house in an hour?"

Dr. Patel nodded, even though Agent Thompson couldn't see her. "We'll be there," she said.

As she hung up the phone, Dr. Patel turned to Maya and the others. "We have a meeting with Agent Thompson in an hour," she said. "Let's get moving."

The team nodded, and they set off towards the safe house. As they walked, Dr. Patel couldn't shake the feeling that they were being watched. She looked around, but saw nothing out of the ordinary.

Still, the feeling persisted. And as they approached the safe house, Dr. Patel couldn't help but wonder if they were walking into a trap.

CROSSING THE COSMIC HORIZON

As they entered the safe house, Dr. Patel's eyes scanned the room, searching for any signs of danger. But everything seemed normal. Agent Thompson was waiting for them, a serious expression on his face.

"Dr. Patel, thank you for coming," he said, his voice formal. "I'm sure you're aware of the situation. We need to debrief you and your team as soon as possible."

Dr. Patel nodded, her eyes never leaving Agent Thompson's face. "Of course," she said. "We're ready to cooperate fully."

But as they began the debriefing process, Dr. Patel couldn't shake the feeling that something was off. Agent Thompson seemed nervous, and the other agents in the room seemed to be watching them with an intensity that made Dr. Patel's skin crawl.

And then, just as they were finishing up the debriefing, Dr. Patel saw something that made her blood run cold. A figure, standing in the shadows, watching them with an unblinking gaze.

Dr. Patel's eyes locked onto the figure, and she felt a chill run down her spine. She knew that they were in grave danger, and that they had to get out of there, fast.

Dr. Patel's eyes remained fixed on the figure, her mind racing with thoughts of escape. She knew that they had to get out of there, and fast.

"Agent Thompson, I think we've said enough for now," Dr. Patel said, her voice firm and authoritative.

Agent Thompson looked at her, a hint of surprise in his eyes. "Of course, Dr. Patel," he said. "I think we've covered everything we need to for now."

Dr. Patel nodded, her eyes never leaving the figure. "Good," she said. "Then I think it's time for us to leave."

As they stood up to leave, Dr. Patel's eyes locked onto the figure, and she saw something that made her blood run cold. The figure was holding a small device, a device that looked eerily familiar.

"Maya, I think we have a problem," Dr. Patel whispered, her eyes never leaving the figure.

Maya followed her gaze, and her eyes widened in shock. "That's a neural disruptor," she whispered back. "It's a device that can control people's minds."

Dr. Patel's eyes locked onto the figure, and she knew that they were in grave danger. She knew that they had to get out of there, and fast.

Without hesitation, Dr. Patel grabbed Maya's arm and pulled her towards the door. "We have to get out of here, now," she whispered urgently.

As they reached the door, Dr. Patel could feel the figure's eyes on her, could sense its malevolent presence. She knew that they were running out of time.

With a surge of adrenaline, Dr. Patel pushed open the door and pulled Maya through it. They sprinted down the hallway, the sound of footsteps echoing behind them.

As they ran, Dr. Patel could feel the figure's presence closing in around them. She knew that they were in grave danger, and that they had to keep running if they wanted to survive.

But as they turned a corner, Dr. Patel saw something that made her heart sink. The hallway was blocked by a group of agents, their eyes cold and unyielding.

Dr. Patel's eyes locked onto the agents, and she knew that they were trapped. She knew that they had to think fast if they wanted to escape.

With a surge of adrenaline, Dr. Patel grabbed Maya's arm and pulled her towards the agents. "We have to get through them," she whispered urgently.

Maya nodded, her eyes flashing with determination. "Let's do it," she said.

Together, they charged towards the agents, their hearts pounding with fear. But as they clashed with the agents, Dr. Patel realized that something was off.

CROSSING THE COSMIC HORIZON

The agents seemed to be moving in perfect sync, their movements almost robotic. And as Dr. Patel looked into their eyes, she saw something that made her blood run cold.

They were under mind control.

Dr. Patel's eyes locked onto the agents, and she knew that they were in grave danger. She knew that they had to think fast if they wanted to escape.

But as she looked around, Dr. Patel realized that they were surrounded. The agents were closing in on them from all sides, their eyes cold and unyielding.

Dr. Patel's heart sank, and she knew that they were running out of time. She knew that they had to think fast if they wanted to survive.

But as she looked at Maya, Dr. Patel saw something that gave her hope. Maya was smiling, a fierce determination in her eyes.

"We're not going down without a fight," Maya said, her voice low and deadly.

Dr. Patel nodded, a surge of adrenaline coursing through her veins. "Let's do it," she said.

Together, they charged towards the agents, their hearts pounding with fear. But as they clashed with the agents, Dr. Patel realized that they were in for the fight of their lives.

As they fought against the agents, Dr. Patel and Maya quickly realized that they were outnumbered and outgunned. The agents were too strong, too fast, and too well-coordinated.

Despite their best efforts, they were slowly but surely being pushed back. The agents were too powerful, and Dr. Patel and Maya were starting to tire.

Just when it seemed like all was lost, the lead agent, Agent Thompson, stepped forward and grabbed Dr. Patel and Maya, holding them in a tight grip.

"It's over," Agent Thompson said, his voice firm and commanding. "You're coming with me."

Dr. Patel and Maya struggled against Agent Thompson's grip, but he was too strong. He dragged them away, throwing them into a waiting vehicle.

As they drove away, Dr. Patel and Maya looked at each other in despair. They had been captured, and they had no idea what would happen to them next.

The vehicle drove for what felt like hours, finally stopping at a massive, futuristic complex. Dr. Patel and Maya were dragged out of the vehicle and taken inside, where they were greeted by a group of stern-looking officials.

"Welcome to Cosmic Federation headquarters," one of the officials said, his voice cold and unfriendly. "You are hereby charged with crimes against the Cosmic Federation. You will be held for trial and sentencing."

Dr. Patel and Maya looked at each other in shock and horror. They had been captured, and they were going to be put on trial. But for what? And what would happen to them next?

As they were led away to their cells, Dr. Patel and Maya couldn't help but wonder what the future held for them. Would they be able to clear their names and escape? Or would they be trapped forever, prisoners of the Cosmic Federation?

Only time would tell.

Don't miss out!

Visit the website below and you can sign up to receive emails whenever Anthony Fontenot publishes a new book. There's no charge and no obligation.

https://books2read.com/r/B-A-STPNB-SLPJF

BOOKS 2 READ

Connecting independent readers to independent writers.

Did you love *Crossing The Cosmic Horizon*? Then you should read *Star Line Horizon*[1] by Anthony Fontenot!

A Gripping Space Opera Adventure

In the vast expanse of the galaxy, Captain Deloy and his infamous pirate crew, Maverick's Revenge, embark on a daring mission to take down the Aurora Cosmic Federation's prized vessel, Aurora's Hope.

With cunning hacks, precision sabotage, and fearless boarding, Deloy's crew must outwit and outmaneuver the Federation's elite forces.

As tensions rise and allegiances blur, Deloy's pirates forge unlikely alliances, confront rival enemies and face impossible choices that threaten the very fabric of the galaxy.

---

1. https://books2read.com/u/bOqDp0

2. https://books2read.com/u/bOqDp0

Join the Maverick's Revenge on their perilous quest for supremacy in the lawless cosmos.

high-stakes adventure

Space Opera

Read more at www.tiktok.com/@a.cosmic.horizon.

About the Author

A born and raised Texan, Anthony Fontenot will usually introduce himself as "basically Hank Hill". The casual observer may note that he has a very nice beard, unlike his animated counterpart. He collects VHS tapes, specifically of the horror and sci-fi genres. He's worked a myriad of jobs, his favorite being part of the team at Ripley's Believe It Or Not!, as well as being a light and sound technition for local and touring major music artists. He currently makes his living as a security guard. He enjoys making art, going to concerts, and spending time with family and friends.

Read more at www.tiktok.com/@a.cosmic.horizon.

www.ingramcontent.com/pod-product-compliance
Ingram Content Group UK Ltd.
Pitfield, Milton Keynes, MK11 3LW, UK
UKHW041942131224
452403UK00004B/365